When Heroes Rise

When Heroes Rise

Trever Bierschbach

Copyright © 2019 Gray Raven Press

Cover Photograph by Patrick Tomasso

All Rights Reserved.

ISBN: 978-1-7335590-0-3

This collection is dedicated to my family, Julie and Gavin, who have supported me through all the years of writing and dreaming. They've made this all possible.

Table of Contents

Introduction 1

Knight's Battle Prayer 3

By Blade and Bow 4

Home is Where the Soul Is 17

Goodbye, I Love You 38

Sam 44

Wastelander 64

Wastelander: Not as They Appear 95

The Healer's Burden: A Wasteland Tale 113

Relic Hunter: A Wasteland Tale 153

Introduction

A hero is someone who puts others before themselves, often risking their own lives to defend, protect, and save others. Heroes can come from all walks of life, and aren't always people. Sometimes a hero is a person whose job requires them to run into burning buildings, other times they're just regular people faced with irregular circumstances. They make a hard decision, run headlong into danger, and sometimes pay the ultimate sacrifice for their trouble.

When Heroes Rise is a collection of short stories about heroes, set in the world of Thelos. These stories will span millennia and more as we experience the life of heroes from the world's magical past, to its post-apocalyptic future. This is a world of magic, technology, adventure, and excitement. It is unlike any world you've visited before so sit back and enjoy this journey through time with a few of the heroes of Thelos. There's one extra short set in our own world thrown in the middle because I think it fits the theme of brave people struggling and giving for the sake of others.

Knight's Battle Prayer

As Gavin Dragonwing

Bleak is the color of our misfortune,
Pale and devoid of life.
Great is the price of our redemption,
Perilous and wrought with strife.

Glorious is the power in our creation,
Strong and full of light.
Disaster is the effect of our destruction,
Merciless and burning bright.

Hot is the fire of our passion,
Fierce and quick of breath.
Now is the time of our salvation,
Swift and honorable in death.

By Blade and Bow

The late afternoon sun was warm as its light filtered down through the trees. The leaves of the towering oaks flared like millions of sparkling emeralds in the rays of light. The shadows and light played across the painted face of the elven man sitting on a log in front of a small elf girl. Both the man and girl were dressed in leathers that mimicked the colors of the woodland around them. A beautiful elven woman sat next to him and all around were the sounds of the Shah'vin clanhold, hidden among the trees of the Great Wood. The girl, Snowdove, quietly studied the loving face of her father while he laughed and talked with her mother. Honesty and love is what she saw there, and pride in his family. The love she saw there was pure and strong as the boles of the oaks around them. The Shah'vin tend to have many lovers before they are bonded, but once they do bind their soul to another it becomes the only romantic relationship of their life.

The Shah'vin were a tribal people that revered the forest and creatures that lived in it. They were dark of skin and hair, and tattooed their faces and bodies with intricate patterns representing the animal spirits they held dear. They lived off the land around but always gave thanks to the spirits of the animals that supplied their food and clothing. To other people the elves seemed savage or uncivilized, with feathers and stones braided into their hair, and their clothing of rough skins and furs. They were a xenophobic people who rarely dealt with outsiders and defended their territory with harsh impunity. There was little trade with outsiders but when they did it was often for metalcraft, weapons and tools they had no desire or skill to make on their own.

Grayfalcon, Snow's father, was a warden of the territory of the Shah'vin clan. Outside the clan he would have been known as a ranger or woods guide, but to the Shah'vin, warden meant so much more. The wardens patrolled the forest around the clanhold, keeping an eye out for those who would threaten the land or her people. They were also the messengers that kept contact with other clans in the Great Wood, and they were war leaders when the need arose. Her mother, Shiningdoe, was a shaman of the clan, a priestess to outsiders. It was no mystery that Snowdove was closest to her father.

"Snowdove?" Her father's voice brought her out of her reverie.

"Yes, Papa?" The little elf asked with a smile and settled her eyes on the familiar face that was painted with symbols to look like a bird of prey.

"Have you been practicing with the bow I made for you?"

"Yes, Papa," she said excitedly, looking down at the small bow that never seemed to leave her side.

When she came of age, and if she trained as a warden, she would craft her own warbow. It was the only time the Shah'vin took live wood from the forest, in a sacred ceremony to honor the spirit of the Great Wood. Even their homes were created using a ritual that asked the trees to grow and change to provide shelter for the clan. In this way the elves literally lived as one with the Great Wood. Her bow was made from a young tree that fell in a storm, but to her it was as good as any true warbow.

"Grayfalcon, what did I tell you about wasting her time? She will follow me in service to the Gods," Shiningdoe whispered urgently. Snowdove made a face that only Grayfalcon could see and it made him smile.

"Do not worry love," Grayfalcon patted his mate's knee, "She has plenty of time to learn both."

Shiningdoe stood abruptly, brushing the warden's hand off, and stalked away. With a sigh Grayfalcon turned to his daughter.

"Papa, I want to be a warden like you," Snowdove said firmly.

"You have plenty of time to figure out your own path, Little Bird. You can do whatever you wish to do in your life."

"I want to go out on patrol with you, Papa. I have been practicing a lot," Snowdove said plaintively.

"I am sorry Snow, you are too young yet, and with the tarquil moving deeper into the Wood again it is too dangerous."

"How many *tarquil* have you killed, Papa?" She said the word with disgust. Tarquil were related to elves but they thrived on warfare and the domination of others, where her people valued life and peace. The tarquil especially enjoyed enslaving others who they believed were weak and inferior. Their slaves were forced into service in the tarquil army to be fodder before the regular forces.

"Snowdove! Never take pride in killing, even our enemies have souls. The People respect all life, even when we are forced to take it," Grayfalcon said firmly.

"Yes, Papa," Snowdove said quietly, lowering her eyes. Grayfalcon reached out to take Snowdove in his arms. She melted into the safety and comfort of her father's embrace.

"Papa, where did they come from? The tarquil I mean," Snowdove asked.

"You know this story Little Bird," Grayfalcon said with a smile.

"I know Papa. I want to hear it again."

The warden leaned back against a nearby tree and held his daughter close. She sighed contentedly, resting her head against his chest.

"As you know, the keepers tell us that all of the People sprang from nature. We, and the other clans around, came from the trees. That is why we protect the Great Wood, that is our mother, and our sibling spirits that live here. There are some clans that sprang from the deer, or the hawk. Some elves even rose from the land itself, but the tarquil sprang from the panther. They were much like us in ages past, but they took up the study of magic," the warden spoke softly, reciting the story he had told so many times. At the mention of the word magic, Snowdove made a face like she had eaten something foul.

"The magic they studied turned dark," the elder elf continued. "It corrupted them, changing them to look like the great cat. Eventually their magic summoned a powerful daemon who turned the tarquil from our Gods and enslaved them. The daemon demanded they wage war on the whole world, so they fight endlessly in their madness. That is why we always watch, Little Bird, to protect our clan from the lost ones."

"Will they ever be good again?" Snowdove asked, as she always did when he recited the tale.

"Some believe there can be tarquil who are goodly. Every one I've seen is twisted and evil, but the world is a full of surprises."

Snowdove smiled and held tighter to her father. The sun was going down and the evening was turning out to be a perfect one, as far as she was concerned. They stayed that way for several minutes before an alarm was raised. Horns called from the nearby woods and several wardens could be seen gathering their weapons and moving toward the sound.

"What is it?" Grayfalcon asked a passing warden.

"Tarquil, attacking the Dah'vae clanhold," the elf responded before disappearing into the trees, headed east.

The Dah'vae were the closest clan to the Shah'vin. Long-time allies, the two clans assisted each other without question. Every elf of both clans knew, if one was in danger it would soon reach the other. The clans were as reliant on each other as they were on the land.

"I must go Little Bird," Grayfalcon said calmly. He hugged her tight to his chest before putting her down and taking up his warbow. Without a backward glance, he vanished into the Great Wood with the other wardens.

*   *   *

Something was wrong in the Great Wood, something that the Shah'vin wardens should have noticed. In their urgency to get to the Dah'vae territory however, they missed it. The Dah'vae had suffered many losses over the last couple of months of tarquil raids, and the Shah'vin elders agreed to assist in any way they could. A small group of wardens worked as a relay message system so if there was need the Shah'vin could spring to action. The Shah'vin were near the border with their neighbor clan when that 'something' became lethally apparent. A gurgling scream told Grayfalcon that his forward scout had met the enemy. It was impossible to tell who was wounded, but they would soon find out. As the wardens moved toward the sound a large group of dark-clad figures rushed through the trees toward them.

"Ambush!" Grayfalcon shouted. He dropped his bow and drew his blades.

Grayfalcon wielded a curved scimitar, paired with a bent-bladed kukri. Both were expensive for the Shah'vin, and he'd paid a passing trader handsomely for them. He, and the other wardens, dove for cover as a hail of arrows fell among them. If not for their keen hearing, they would have missed the twang of bowstrings and been cut down where they stood. The wardens needed no direction. There were no commands and each elf drew his preferred close-combat weapon and rushed to attack. They moved as a pack, reading each other's body language, and anticipating the movement of their closest ally so that each supported the others without need for signals or words.

When Grayfalcon came out from behind his cover he faced an attacker who wielded a wickedly curved falchion in both hands. The warden could see his enemy's pale hair and fur, as well as his silver eyes that reflected the dim moonlight. His feline features were twisted in a snarling rage as he bared his sharp teeth at the elf. The sight of the clan's long-time enemy was all the motivation Grayfalcon needed. A primal growl escaped him as he sprang to attack.

The warden's initial strike was blocked by the tarquil warrior, who responded with a powerful overhand swing. Grayfalcon knew his blade was no match for the heavier falchion so he caught it with his sword at an angle that sent the large weapon wide. His enemy stumbled forward with the momentum. The warden took advantage of the misstep and brought the razor-sharp edge of his kukri up to meet the neck of his foe. The curved blade caught and held the tarquil for the briefest of moments before the warden stepped past him and relaxed his wrist. The dying tarquil slid off the blade sporting a new smile across his throat.

A quick look around showed the dire peril the Shah'vin were in. Grayfalcon had been the only one lucky enough to encounter a single foe. The rest of the wardens were facing two or three to one odds. He was thankful to note that all of the wardens in his charge were still alive, but there were too many tarquil. Grayfalcon signaled a withdrawal with a powerful whistle that pierced the sounds of clashing steel and the screams of the injured and dying. The wardens retreated while Grayfalcon tried to take some of the attention of the attackers. The tarquil's lesser experience with the terrain helped the Shah'vin as they seemed to melt into the brush, disappear behind trees, and come together in twos and threes, always moving west toward their clanhold. Their fastest runner had already taken it upon herself to get back to the village quickly and warn the rest of the clan.

The quick disappearance of their enemy left the tarquil confused and angry. The only reason they hesitated in pursuing was one lone elf that stood in plain view of the raiders. They were amused by his bravado and confident they could chase down, and eliminate the rest after seeing how this played out. Grayfalcon watched the enemy calmly, his sword and kukri relaxed, his knees slightly bent, and every nerve in his body on edge and ready.

"He is mine, we will take care of the rest soon," one of the tarquil said in his own language. Grayfalcon was unfamiliar with the tongue, but the meaning was clear. The speaker stepped forward and his comrades relaxed, talking excitedly.

Grayfalcon allowed his enemy to come to him. The warden studied his adversary, from his relaxed stride to his intent gaze. This one is dangerous, the elf thought, dangerous and unafraid. The tarquil was armored as his companions were, in a fine chain mail with decorative leather panels over the shoulders and chest. Under his armor was a simple tunic and his legs were protected by leather greaves over leather sandals. His weapons included a slim longsword in his right hand, and on his left, a spiked gauntlet that seemed more weapon than protection.

A wicked smile spread across the tarquil's face, revealing his pointed cat-like teeth. His slitted silver eyes shined as he approached. With no warning in his eyes or body the tarquil's sword came up and out, aimed at Grayfalcon's chest. The warden was prepared and easily deflected the blow with his kukri. He followed up the attack with one of his own, swinging his scimitar for the other's neck, but the tarquil knocked the blade aside with his gauntlet. The two traded blows for several minutes, circling, attacking, parrying, but neither seemed to get the upper hand.

The opportunity that Grayfalcon was waiting for presented itself, as the tarquil stumbled on an exposed root and put his gauntleted hand out for balance. Their swords were locked again so the warden crossed over with his kukri to hit his enemy in the face. The warden realized too late that the stumble had been a feint. The tarquil brought his steel-clad fist up to meet the attack. Their fists connected and the warden could hear the bones in his hand crack as his fingers were crushed between the steel gauntlet and his own kukri hilt. A scream escaped his throat and the blade fell to the ground. The elf stumbled back, holding his arm close to his body to shield his ruined hand.

The tarquil smiled and advanced, giving the Shah'vin no time to recover. Grayfalcon was desperate now. He had to buy his warriors time to get back to defend the village and it was clear that this tarquil was playing with him. The warden had to keep his enemy interested.

Grayfalcon leaped to the attack before the tarquil could raise his sword. He hoped to catch his enemy by surprise, and it worked, to an extent. The feline warrior managed only to deflect the point of the scimitar from his chest to his shoulder. The tarquil growled in pain and anger, and swung his gauntleted fist at the warden's head. The glancing blow knocked the elf to the ground. Grayfalcon rose unsteadily to his feet and the tarquil grabbed him by the throat, driving the point of his sword into the elf's bicep.

"How do you like that, bark eater?" The tarquil asked in heavily accented trade common.

The vicious tarquil pushed harder, twisting his blade and smiling when Grayfalcon screamed. The warden tried to raise his sword with his impaled arm, but the tarquil pulled his own blade free and took hold of the warden's wrist with the hand that had been choking the elf. The tarquil chuckled as he casually swung his sword and parted the warden's arm at the elbow. He kicked the stunned elf to the ground. Grayfalcon could barely hear the other tarquil around him laughing over the rush of blood in his ears.

"This will be slow," the tarquil whispered. He stabbed the warden in the stomach, and then twisted his blade free.

* * *

A few injured elves stumbled out of the trees while Snowdove watched anxiously. Most of the patrol had made it back and were quickly organizing a defense of the clanhold. Snowdove knew all of the wardens like she knew her own hands and she watched and counted. There were two left to return, Foxfire, and her father. Her mother was already helping the injured, so Snowdove waited and watched alone. The little elf felt fear rise up in her stomach when Foxfire finally exited the forest. Foxfire stumbled as if she had been running forever. The warden's hair and clothing were tattered and tangled with leaves, and there were tears freely streaming down her face.

"Snow, where is your mother?" Foxfire gasped.

"I don't know. Where is Papa?" Snowdove asked, fear creeping into her voice.

Foxfire started to walk away to look for Shiningdoe but the sound of Snowdove's voice made her stop. She looked down and touched the little elf's cheek.

"He is gone Little Bird," the warden said quietly.

"Papa!" That one word, full of so much anguish, pain, fear, and grief tore at Foxfire's heart. The little elf turned to run into the forest but Foxfire caught her in a tight embrace. Snowdove beat her small fists against the warden's back.

"You are lying! Where is Papa?" She screamed.

"No little one, I saw Grayfalcon fall. He stayed behind so we could get back to protect the People," Foxfire explained.

Snowdove sobbed until she was too weak to raise her arms. The warden held her tight until she calmed down, and then held her out to look into the little elf's eyes.

"Now Snowdove, I need you to do something for me. I am going to find your mother and tell her what happened. I need you to go find all of the young ones and get them to the center of the clanhold and keep them safe," Snowdove nodded and set out without a word or backward glance.

* * *

Nothing would ever be the same for Snowdove. The tarquil had been driven off by the defenders, and her father's body was recovered. His warbow was lost but his blades were given to Shiningdoe to keep for Snowdove. Her father was gone and she would have to get used to that. Her mother was so busy with the grove, and negotiating with a white dragon that had moved into their territory. Snowdove spent her time with the other wardens when they were in the clanhold, and was determined to follow her father's path of protecting the Great Wood with blade and bow.

Home is Where the Soul Is

The young elf woman sat in the leaves at the base of the massive oak she lived in with her mother. She held a small, pink gemstone that was attached to a leather cord around her neck. Her bronze-skinned fingers moved across the surface of the stone, seeking some remnant of the piece of her father's soul that once resided there.

Soulstones, as they were known to the Shah'vin, were part of the bond formed when two elves chose to be life mates. With the bonding ritual, a piece of their souls became part of the stone, manifesting as a tiny light in the facets of the gem. The bonded would feel a pull as the stones were drawn to each other. It was also how they would find each other beyond the veil. If one of the bonded were to die the mate would remain unbonded until they too passed beyond and their souls would be drawn together. A dark stone meant the wearer was already beyond, waiting for their lover. Elves bond forever and, while they may have many lovers after their bondmate dies, it was unheard of for them to bond again.

She was surrounded by the sounds of the Wood and the clanhome. The wind through the trees, the chatter of the animals and birds, and the soft voices of her clan was something she always found comforting. She liked to think of her father when the world around was at peace, it seemed fitting after the violent death he suffered. She leaned her head back against the bark of the tree, trying to bring his face to mind. It was becoming difficult to recall his voice or his features as each year passed. Unfortunately, her peace was short lived.

"There you are Snowdove, it's time for your studies," Shiningdoe stopped a few feet away. She was standing with a white-haired elven male, her hand resting on his arm.

The man's eyes were icy blue and his skin was pale. He wasn't an elf at all, but a white dragon shifted into elf form. The dragon had lived near the clan for some time and Shiningdoe was tasked with being the contact between the clan and dragon. The task had obviously developed into more than being the clan's emissary. Snowdove frowned at the two and tucked the stone into her shirt. She stood and adjusted her father's blades she wore on her hip. Shiningdoe shook her head in disapproval.

"Why do you carry those? Shaman do not carry blades," Snow's mother said shortly.

"Some of us try to remember him," Snow said coldly, looking down at her mother's hand on the dragon's arm, then back to her eyes. She could see the affect of her words as her mother's eyes turned hard and angry.

"Snowdove," her mother said sternly but it was too late.

Satisfied that her barb hit home, the young elf turned on her heel and walked away. Snowdove had no desire to be a shaman so she took her time getting to the healing grove for her studies. While she walked through the clanhome two young elf males approached her. The two were dressed in the green and brown leathers of wardens, though she knew they had yet to pass their trials and training.

"Snow, off to the healing grove?" Stormcrow, the taller of the two asked.

"Unfortunately," Snowdove growled.

"You should come with us, we're headed up to the lake," Silverwolf, the other young elf said, stepping up to take Stormcrow's hand.

Snowdove looked toward her destination, considering how her mother would be if she skipped her lessons to run off with her friends. She wondered if she cared how angry Shiningdoe would be. The decision was an easy one.

"Let's go," she said, leading them north, toward the lake.

They reached the lake near midday and wasted no time stripping off their leathers and jumping into the clear water. The lake was deep, making the water cold, but they were thankful for it. The forest was stuffy under the summer sun. Snowdove surfaced near her friends after diving deep to get used to the cold. She wiped the water from her eyes and dragged her fingers through her shoulder-length hair.

"When are you going to tell your mother you're going to start training with the wardens?" Stormcrow asked.

"She'll find out soon enough, if she hasn't already," Snowdove said, treading water calmly with the other two.

"Snow, it will go better if you tell her yourself," Silverwolf said.

"I don't care Silverwolf. Have you seen her with that dragon? She hangs onto Ketalax like they are already bonded!" She shouted the last, expelling the anger she had been feeling since seeing the two together that morning.

Her friends looked at each other grimly. They, like all Shah'vin, understood the importance of bonding. It was something the two had talked about themselves but neither was ready for the commitment.

"Perhaps they are just lovers," Silverwolf offered.

"Perhaps," Snowdove conceded.

Stormcrow broke the tension by darting his hand under the water and pinching Silverwolf. That act caused a playful retaliation that quickly turned into a wrestling match. Snowdove's anger evaporated and she smiled, splashing both of them before turning away. She left the lovers to their sport and swam lazily across the lake.

Reaching the far shore Snowdove climbed out of the water and shivered when the breeze blew across her wet skin. She walked along the water's edge confidently despite being unarmed, unclothed, alone alone in the Wood. They were still well within Shah'vin territory. She knew there would be a patrol of wardens nearby.

The young elf walked through the tall grasses between the water and trees and thought about her future. She wanted nothing more than to follow her father's path and join the wardens. She also knew her mother would not approve. She was committed to her course, but she was certain that defying her mother on this would widen the rift that already existed between them. She was set on her decision to become a warden, but she hoped she would be able to find a way to break it to her mother without losing her completely.

The young elf woman moved toward the trees, enjoying the feel of the hot sun on her skin. The late summer blooms washed the field with a vast array of colors and smells, and her ears were filled with the sound of thousands of insects going about their daily tasks. She was so distracted by her thoughts she failed to notice the ridgeback cub until it was nearly too late.

Ridgebacks were similar to bears, The People believe they were the ancestors of the common bear that roamed the land. Ridgebacks were a rare sight in the Great Wood. The cub was already larger than any bear. She guessed he was less than a year old but he was already close to the height of the grass all around them, the tops of which brushed Snow's shoulders. His bony ridges were still small but would be deadly if he wanted them to be. His head was that of a bear but much larger with bony ridges above his eyes. His fur was dark brown and thick, and his paws were a testament to the massive size he would reach in a few years. He, like all ridgebacks, was built for power. Most of his strength would be in the large front legs and massive shoulders. His back sloped down to smaller hind legs, with claws that were equally deadly.

Snow watched the powerful beast chase a butterfly and smiled despite the danger she knew she was in. Mother ridgeback would be close. Snow was drawn to watch the large, and still ungainly, creature attempt to stalk the brightly colored insect. The ridgeback cub leaped and crashed through the grasses, trying but failing to catch his prey. The butterfly, oblivious to its pursuer, flew a lazy path that eventually brought it to land on a flower a few feet in front of Snowdove.

The young elf realized her peril too late. She was so mesmerized by the sight of the ridgeback that she hardly moved when the insect landed nearby. She looked down at the patterned orange and black wings, then back up to where the cub had been. The cub was also intently watching the insect but his own instincts made him raise his head the moment Snow turned her eyes to him.

When their eyes met, they both froze. Neither could look away as a storm of emotions engulfed them. Both experienced fear but were unable to run, they were both curious but too scared to move closer. There was another emotion, a feeling of being drawn to each other. To Snow, the feeling was something between the friendship she felt for the two swimming in the lake and the love for her father. The moment, for the two of them, seemed to last an eternity. That eternity was shattered as soon as it began by a terrifying roar above them. Snowdove and the cub both looked up to see mamma ridgeback towering over them, voicing her displeasure at the chance meeting. The female stood twice as tall as Snow, with massive bony spines running from the base of her skull and over her shoulders. The beast's paws were larger than the elf's head and its jaws and teeth that could bite Snow in two.

Snow took one last look at the cub, who was staring at her and backing slowly away. The young elf knew better than to push her luck. She turned and fled for the lake with mama ridgeback's roar chasing her through the tall grass. She hit the water hard and paused to take a breath before putting her head down and swimming for the far shore and her friends. When she got there Silverwolf and Stormcrow looked at her curiously as she approached through the water.

"What did you stir up over there, Little Bird?" Stormcrow asked, nodding in the direction she'd come from.

"Ridgeback mother and cub," Snow gasped between breaths.

The two looked at her with astonishment and Silverwolf pulled her close and turned her around in the water.

"How were you not mauled?" Silverwolf asked while he looked her over for injury.

"I ran. She stayed with the cub," Snow answered.

"I don't believe any Shah'vin has escaped a ridgeback, caught in the open, naked and defenseless," Stormcrow said, wonder in his voice.

"Perhaps Snowdove is too scrawny to look appetizing," Silverwolf smiled and pinched her backside. The trio erupted into shouts and splashing as Snow fended off the other two. The playful fight soon degenerated into a free-for-all match of wrestling and dunking.

*   *   *

Snow lay in the soft moss under a massive oak near the edge of the clanhome. The sunlight was warm through the leaves, but the shadows kept the air cool. To an observer it might look as if she were asleep but she was aware of every tiny ray of light playing warmly across her skin as the leaves moved in the breeze. She was imagining the ridgeback cub, thinking about what it would be like to wander the Wood with him close. To run through the open glades with such a beast as her companion, to feel his warm fur under her hands, and his deep breaths in the dark when they slept. She imagined the wonder it would cause in the clanhome with him at her side. Her mother would be unable to deny her path if she bonded so young to such a powerful animal totem.

"Snowdove!" Her mother's voice cut through the young elf's reverie. From the sound of it, Shiningdoe had tried to get her attention more than once. Snow looked up at her mother's angry eyes, then past her to the eyes of the dragon that was masquerading as an elf.

"You did not appear for your lessons today," Her mother said brusquely. "Were you following one of the wardens around again?"

"I was not following a patrol," Snow said. She was angry about being disturbed and surprised at how deep she had been in the daydream.

"Where were you then?" Shiningdoe asked, clearly irritated by Snow's distracted state.

"We went to the lake, Silverwolf, Stormcrow and I," she could see her mother's lips tighten in anger. "I saw a ridgeback cub."

"The lake?" Her mother began, her voice rising, "You will be a poor healer if you continue to avoid your instruction."

Snow sighed, getting to her feet, "I do not want to be a healer."

"You've let your friends fill your head…"

"Something happened out there, mother," Snow interrupted. "When I looked into the ridgeback's eyes, I felt something."

"His eyes?" Fear now crept into Shiningdoe's voice, "You could have been killed."

Snow thought she heard genuine concern in her mother's voice. That moment was broken when her mother's companion spoke.

"Snowdove, you should mind your mother's wishes. If your father were here…," he began.

"No!" The young elf screamed at him, "Don't you ever speak of my father. You do not know what he would want."

Shiningdoe reached out to her daughter. Snow jerked away.

"I am going to train with the wardens. Deal with that as you will mother," Snow spat the last word out as if it were sour fruit. She stormed away, angry that the dragon has presumed to speak for her father but angrier still that her mother had let him.

*   *   *

Snow began her training as a warden that autumn and had little time for anything else. Shiningdoe had tried again to convince her to follow the shaman's path, but Snow made it clear that, short of tying her up, there was no chance of her returning to those studies. Most of her time was spent in the company of one warden or another, learning to hunt, track, and pass through the Wood undetected.

When she did have time away from training, she spent much it at the north lake, looking for any sign of the ridgeback cub. Sometimes her friends joined her but often she went alone. She still had difficulty explaining the feelings she was having, or the pull she felt that made her try to find the cub again.

When winter hit, and she knew hibernation would ensure no sightings of the cub, she stopped going to the lake. Despite that, she found herself constantly thinking of the cub, and the events of that summer day. Finally, she decided to talk to the one person she trusted as much as she had her father, the warden Foxfire.

"So, tell me what's on your mind Little Bird," Foxfire asked when they were well away from the clanhome. Snowdove had insisted they speak in private.

"Have you heard of anyone, in all the clans, that has bonded with an animal?" Snow asked. Saying the words out loud made her feel sillier than she had when she first had the thought.

"Well, of course. Several of the wardens have made friends of animals," Foxfire began.

"No, not pets like Nightowl's falcon. A real bond, the kind you feel in your soul."

"Snow, the sort of bond you speak of hasn't happened for generations and even then, it was very rare," Foxfire explained.

"That's as I thought. I hoped that maybe the wardens had heard otherwise from a distant clan," Snow said, unsure of her suspicions now.

"Little Bird, what's all this about? I get the feeling there is more to your questions than simple curiosity," Foxfire asked.

Snow considered telling the warden about her experience with the ridgeback. Foxfire had been like another parent to her after her father was killed and the younger elf trusted the warden more than anyone she knew. Finally, she decided to confide in her oldest friend. She told

Foxfire everything, even her suspicions about the feelings she had during the encounter.

"Gods, Little Bird, you are lucky to be alive," the warden said in amazement.

"I know, but I am alive and I am trying to make sense of these feelings," Snow said, sounding desperate for an answer.

"It sounds like a true bonding like we've heard in the old tales," Foxfire said.

Snow nodded, excited by what seemed to be confirmation of her thoughts, but also scared.

"You haven't encountered the cub on your return visits?" Foxfire asked.

"No," Snow confirmed.

"It's probably for the best, your father would never forgive me if I let you get eaten by mama ridgeback," the warden said with a smile.

Snowdove smiled and nodded at that. She stopped short of saying she would abandon her search though. She refused to make a promise she knew she would break.

* * *

When spring finally bloomed in the Great Wood, Snowdove again started frequenting the area she had seen the ridgebacks. Springtime was always her favorite time of year. The Wood was so alive after the long sleep of winter. The sights and sounds of animals and birds mixed with the scents of plants blooming into new life were all around her. The young elf began to venture further from the lake on her excursions to find the cub. She hoped he would recognize her and wondered how large he had grown over the winter. Snow listened to the singing birds in the trees as she walked along, looking for any sign of the cub. This area of the Wood was foreign to her and she was becoming nervous.

As she traveled the sounds of animals faded away to silence deeper in the thick stands of ancient trees. The lack of sound washed over her and she stopped in her tracks. The forest animals would know a ridgeback and carry on as normal. Something was different. The area around the clanhome had been peaceful for years so she only carried her bow and few arrows. She was alone, and too remote to call for help.

Snow was on alert as she moved deeper into the unfamiliar Wood. The silence in the trees was like an alarm in her head. If the cub did not recognize her or it was a different ridgeback, she could be in considerable danger. What did burst out of the underbrush caught her so off guard that she had no time to raise her bow to defend herself.

At first glance, the creature looked like a small bear, covered in brown fur and moving on two legs. It was moving too fast to be a bear though, a realization Snow made too late. The large human came at her, swinging a club at her head. She tried to dodge but only managed to turn the killing blow into one that knocked her senseless. The last sight she saw before darkness took her was the huge man leering down at her through his shaggy beard.

*   *   *

They kept her locked up for days, or was it a month, in the hut. Her only furnishing was the waste bucket she was loath to use but did so out of necessity. Her only comfort was the dirt floor, a connection to the land. She stayed in the middle of the hut, as far away from the dead tree walls as she could. Barely conscious, tired, hungry and in pain, Snowdove was a prisoner of one of the human tribes that lived in the northern mountains that bordered the Great Wood.

The Shah'vin had little contact with the barbarians. They rarely entered elven territory. When they did they were easily driven off by the wardens. What little the Shah'vin did know was the humans were primitive and savage, and worshipped animal totems. They tended to adopt one totem for the entire tribe. From what she could tell, Snow was captive of the bear tribe, known to be one of the most brutal in the region. They fed her once a day, mostly meat but she left it untouched. Her people ate the meat of animals, but only after giving thanks to the spirit of the animal that gave its life for them. Sometimes they would bring bread or nuts that she would pick at if she had the strength. Strength was something she was losing rapidly and it was clear the barbarians were only interested in keeping her alive as long as her body held out. She was no more than a curiosity to them.

In her captivity, she was frequently beaten and raped, used for whatever sadistic desire the men of the tribe had for her. The women would come in and clean her up between visits from the men, but they looked on her like she was an animal and none took pity on her. Their only concern was to keep her breathing. The one she called Bear, since the first mistaken encounter, was her primary abuser. He seemed to have more than a passing fascination with his captive and he expressed it by being the most vicious of her tormentors.

For the moment all was quiet in her prison and that was when her ordeal was the hardest to handle. Fear and dread set in. Uncertainty about when they would come next, or which one of them it would be, ate at her in the dark. At least when she was being tortured, she had an outlet for the emotions, someone in which to direct her hate. Alone, her emotions turned inward and they were always dark.

She could think of a dozen ways to end it, but suicide was unconscionable to a people who revered all life. Even so, she still considered giving up and letting the darkness take her. She berated herself endlessly for being so careless to be captured by a human. She questioned her own feelings about the ridgeback that had led her to such a foolhardy act. She tried to block the dark thoughts, and many times she was successful with prayer or thoughts of her father. It never lasted long before the pain would overcome her and break her concentration.

The day she finally knew would be her last came to her without any surprise or sorrow. She awoke, sore and hungry as usual and lying on the same dirt floor. It was like every other day but somehow she knew. A sense of peace washed over her and the pain melted away. She felt her father close, waiting for her on the other side.

"Soon," she whispered.

She rolled onto her side, using the last of her strength to lift her face off of the dirt. Opening her swollen eyes, she could make out the walls of her prison in the gloom. She was alone, not that she cared anymore. Her ordeal was almost over and she finally felt a sense of relief. When the crude door to her prison was opened and let in the morning light, she hardly registered it. Her only movement was to close her eyes against the painful glare, and lay her head back on the ground.

"Stekka," the man's voice came roughly to her ears. She knew it was Bear; he was the only one that called her that. The word's meaning was foreign to her but she suspected it had something to do with his sense of possession.

She had no fight left when he rolled her on her stomach and puller hips up to meet him. Even if she had the strength she was without the will. She felt as if it was all happening to someone else. A body that was already dead while her soul watched. This was the end, she knew it. She looked upon the young elf's body, her body; clothes long since stripped away, the filthy human thrusting into a vessel that was no longer home to her soul. She felt as if the world was pulling away from her, or she away from it, when the screaming began.

The sound pulled her back, throwing her into a reality she wanted no part of. She was unsure if it the cruel work of the Gods or her own survival instinct, but at that moment she cursed whatever it was. All the peace and detachment she felt disappeared in a flash and the pain came back tenfold.

The screams, and what sounded like the roars of demons, grew closer. She wondered if she was finally losing her mind. Bear seemed oblivious of the commotion she was hearing outside. He continued his abuse of Snow, who added her own screams to those outside now. She tried to fight but the human was too strong and heavy. She felt her body dying. She cursed the Gods for being so cruel as to cast her back into it so she could feel it die.

Snow cried out for something, her father, Foxfire, the Gods, anything. It formed as a primal scream from some ancient part of her soul she had never touched. A thunderous roar accompanied her cry from outside. The roaring increased in intensity as the whole world came apart around Snow.

The young elf saw nothing but the sun hitting the dirt around her. She could hear rending timbers and cracking wood all around. Bear released her suddenly and she collapsed to the ground and rolled onto her back. She looked up into a vision of utter horror. A massive form stood above her and Bear, blotting out the sun and dwarfing the large human. The creature must have been all fur and claws but she could make out a few details with the light behind it. The beast roared again as Bear tried to pull up his fur leggings and another roar answered from somewhere behind snow.

With a speed that belied its bulk the huge monster eviscerated Bear in one swipe of its massive claws. Blood and gore sprayed in every direction. Hot blood splashed across Snow's naked skin, but he was too weak and exhausted to care. The monster lowered itself to four legs and snuffled at the bloody corpse between them. With the sun no longer behind the creature, she could see that it was a male ridgeback; a huge male ridgeback.

The ridgeback moved from its recent kill to Snow and at that moment she thought he was going to kill her next. The thought quickly passed when she made eye contact with the beast. She was instantly flooded with thoughts of protection and love. He had found her when she needed him most.

"It's you," she said in wonder, reaching out to bury her fingers in the fur of his neck as he snuffled at her. She found great comfort in the warmth and strength she felt under that fur.

The ridgeback pressed his nose under her and laid his chest on the ground. She used the last of her strength to pull herself across his shoulders. The softness of his fur was soothing against her battered body. Before closing her eyes to welcome unconsciousness, she saw the destruction caused by the two savage creatures. They must have attacked as the sun rose. The time when most of the humans were rising from their rest. The village stood no chance against the feral monstrosities. Huts were demolished and the few that had managed to raise a defense were torn apart. Women, children, and the old were left alive, and they cowered among the ruins. As far as she could tell, anyone who raised a weapon that morning was dead.

"Take me home," Snow said weakly before she let herself slip into sleep.

*   *   *

Snowdove awoke inside the healer's hall within the largest tree in the clanhome. Foxfire was close to her hammock and she could see her mother hovering some distance away with her silver-haired companion. Snow's entire body hurt but she knew she was healing and would live. She was wrapped tightly in furs and leafy bandages packed with healing poultices. She turned her head and tried to talk but her mouth was too dry to get anything out.

"Relax Little Bird," Foxfire said, giving her a cup of water and helping her drink.

"How long?" Snow finally managed to ask after emptying the cup.

"Your large friend brought you in three days ago. You've been gone over a tenday," Foxfire said.

They all turned at the sound of a loud gruffing coming from outside and Foxfire smiled.

"He's hardly left the side of the hall since he brought you here. He's caused quite a stir," The older warden said. "Silverwolf and Stormcrow have had good company in their vigil."

"Where are they?" Snow wanted to see her friends but from somewhere deep inside the thought filled her with unexplainable dread.

Foxfire looked at her sadly, "They won't come in, I'm sorry Little Bird. When they first visited the sound of their voices seemed to cause you some distress. When Stormcrow tried to comfort you his touch set you to thrashing and screaming. We had to restrain you so you didn't hurt yourself."

A wave of terror and pain swept over Snow and she grit her teeth to keep from crying out. The cool, soft hand on her forehead helped her relax. Foxfire brushed the hair back from her face and held her other hand tightly.

"It's going to be some time before these feelings will fade," Foxfire said.

"Will they ever go away?" Snow asked weakly.

"No one can say Little Bird, but they will fade."

* * *

The feelings of terror did eventually fade but they never went away completely. Snow was in the healer hall another week, days longer than she liked. She could finally stand the presence of the males of her clan but even her two best friends could no longer offer her the comfort of physical contact, especially intimate contact. The thought of lying with a male made her want to claw her skin off. Her mother bonded to the dragon, and Snow took it poorly. When it was announced that she would soon have a sibling she stopped talking to her mother entirely.

She went back to her training sooner than expected but she needed to get out in the Wood, away from so many people. The ridgeback, she called Grimtooth, was always at her side. The elders decided to pair her with a mentor who was also known as a recluse, a young but experienced female warden named Spottedhawk. Snow would feel better away from all the people of her clan. She hated the way she felt, and wondered if she would ever truly feel at home with her clan again.

Goodbye, I Love You

The ribbons of smoke drifted lazily through the air in the old farm house's kitchen. Olive appliances and yellow linoleum showed the ravages of time in the dim glow of the stove light. Ice clinked in a glass of bourbon when the old man set it on the worn tabletop. A lighter clicked and the stranger at the other end of the table lit another expensive cigarette.

"Those are bad for you," the old man said. His voice was weak. Not as strong as it had been years before.

Shoulders shrugged under a black suit coat opposite the old man.

"I'll live," the stranger said. "So to speak."

The stranger's voice sounded bored, like someone who had been working the same job he hated for thirty years.

"Well, they're bad for me then," the old man's cough accentuated his point.

The stranger flicked his ash into an old cut glass ashtray and raised the cigarette to his lips again.

"We both know it's too late for that," the stranger said before taking a drag.

The ashtray was stained with the dregs of many years use, though that night was the first in a long time the old man had pulled it out of the cupboard.

"Why are you here?" The old man asked.

"I've told you why."

"I mean, why now?" The old man asked plaintively. "I'm not ready."

"You've had more time than most," the stranger said.

"I'm scared."

"After all these years? I don't believe you."

The old man looked down at the glass on the table. The stranger was right, he had been a soldier, firefighter, and raised three kids. Little scared him anymore. He was bothered by the stranger, tough. A feeling tugged at the pit of his stomach, but it was something other than fear.

"You've avoided this talk many times over the years," the stranger said. "We can't put it off any longer."

"At Cherbourg," the old man said. His eyes had grown distant and his ears filled with the reports of long-silent guns. Like many of his generation, no amount of time would erase those memories.

"And Bastogne, and that factory on fifth," the stranger said. "Along with a half dozen other times."

The old man shook his head, returning to the present. He lifted the glass with a shaking hand and took a drink. The stranger watched him for a moment as if waiting for him to say something. When the old man remained silent, he snuffed out his cigarette and stood. His chair scraped against the floor as it slid back. The sound caused the old man to start.

"Well, it's time we were on our way," the stranger said.

"Wait."

The stranger paused, a note of interest in his eyes. The light never seemed to hit his face, but his eyes always reflected the glow regardless of where he turned.

"Isn't there something I can give you?" The old man was begging now. "Something I can trade for more time."

"What could you possibly have that I need?"

"I'll give anything."

"Will you?" The stranger asked.

The old man felt a chill creep up his spine. He knew what the stranger dealt in and what his job was. He thought of his wife, his kids, and their kids and he knew he was unwilling to make such a deal.

"No, no I won't," the old man said.

His stooped shoulders slumped in defeat. He steeled himself to stand and leave with the stranger but he stopped and looked at the ceiling.

His wife, of over fifty years, was asleep in their bedroom above. They married after the war and bought the farmhouse they still lived in. Together they raised their children in that house and helped raise many grandchildren there as well. The best memories of over half his life were with his family in their house. In a flash, he knew what it was that had been bothering him.

"Let me say goodbye," he said to the stranger. "Give me one night to tell her I love her."

The stranger looked at him for a few moments. There was no plea this time, just an honest request from the heart. The stranger rarely heard such requests. He nodded and put his cigarettes in his pocket.

"One night," the stranger said and walked to the door. He was gone before the old man could stand and turn around.

The old man finished his drink and set the glass on the counter. He climbed the stairs slowly, grimacing at the pain in his knees and back. The door at the top of the stairs creaked when he pushed it open.

"Couldn't sleep?" His wife asked drowsily.

She rolled toward him and the dim moonlight from the window fell across her features. They were both old. Time, worry, stress, and life had all taken their toll, but he was struck by how beautiful she still was to him.

"What's the matter?" She asked. He was unaware he had been staring.

"Nothing, I just," he stammered, reminded of the first time he saw her. It had taken some time to build up the nerve to go talk to her then. "I love you."

"I love you too, now come to bed. It's cold," she said, shaking her head and smiling at him.

He pulled his feet out of his slippers and climbed under the sheets next to her. She snuggled close and he put his arms around her. She shivered but soon warmed up in his embrace. He laid his head down and took in the scent of her hair, the smell of the shampoo she always used, and perfume she always wore.

"That's better," she said quietly. "Don't go anywhere."

"I'll always be with you, dear," he said.

Her breathing settled into a steady rhythm as she fell asleep again. He lay awake the rest of the night. He listened to the sounds of the old house around them, the world outside, and the steady breathing of his life-long love beside him. Finally, as the dawn began to lighten the drapes he sighed and closed his eyes.

The funeral, two days later, was held during a beautiful afternoon. An old woman stood at a newly dug grave in the middle of a beautiful military cemetery. The old woman was among children and grandchildren, friends and family, while her life-long love was lowered to his rest. She shed no tears, though she was sad. She was thankful he had peace at the end and remembered what he said to her last. He would always be with her.

Her son was walking her to a car when she saw a stranger in a black suit. He was leaning against a tree, smoking an expensive cigarette. She remembered seeing him watching the service.

"Did you know him?" She asked the stranger when they were close.

"We were acquainted," the stranger said. "He was a good man."

The old woman smiled.

"That's kind of you to say. Will you come to the house for coffee?"

"Not today, but I'll call on you before long," the stranger said.

"All right then," she smiled. "You come by soon and we'll swap stories about the old rascal."

He nodded and put the cigarette out under his shoe.

"I wouldn't miss it for anything."

Sam

Sam walked along the broke ground looking for something to eat. He crossed the crumbling pavement where people used to drive their cars before the big flash that changed everything. There weren't any more cars to watch out for, and not many people either. There was a lot less of everything, but Sam thought he saw something move in the field ahead. He crept slowly, watching the tall grass for whatever it was to move again.

Sam saw the rabbit sitting a few feet ahead. He was hungry but he moved patiently. It was difficult for him to find food after he was separated from his family so catching this meal was important. One step at a time he approached within a few feet of his prey. When Sam was close, he pounced on the hare. He was quick and the terrified creature was caught. He was too hungry to wait and tore right into the rabbit with his teeth. He looked around often while he ate. A predator could show up at any time and Sam wanted to be ready. Like the rabbit, the unobservant had short lives.

Sam finished his meal in peace and decided to set his sights on the next priority. Food, water, sleep, all in an endless cycle to survive the blasted world around him. He searched around the area for untainted water, which was no easy task. Rain collected in containers of all types scattered all over the area. That's what Sam searched for. He knew that drinking water that touched the ground could make him sick. After searching for a long time in the heat, Sam found an old metal pot that collected rain from the night before. He got a few swallows of the life-giving liquid that survived evaporation in the shade of a blown-out building. The pavement and blasted ground were becoming uncomfortably hot under the high sun. He crawled under some of the rubble to find a shady spot to rest. With a full belly, he was asleep in no time.

It was dark when Sam heard the voices of people in the distance. It was the first voices he'd heard since being swept downriver after his family was attacked on the bridge. Maybe it was his family. It felt like they'd been separated for most of his life, and he missed them terribly. He felt vulnerable without them. Sam crept out from under the rubble and listened carefully. His sensitive ears quickly located the direction the voices were coming from. He walked out into the dark as the voices grew louder. Sam sensed danger and picked up the pace. He rounded the corner of a crumbling building to find four people facing off over a small fire. He moved into the shadow of the building to watch. The situation didn't look right to him. Two large males were facing another older male and a young female. Sam could feel the younger one's fear.

Sam could make no sense of the argument. The people were clearly angry about something and that made Sam keep his distance. They were strangers, but he had been alone for so long it was nice to hear their voices, despite the tone. The people yelled at each other another minute before one of the angry males pointed at the older one. There was a loud bang and a flash in the dark. The young female screamed and ran, and Sam slid deeper into the shadows as the older man fell to the dirt.

"Should we go after her?" One of the two asked. Sam could hear him as he turned to his companion.

"No, we have their stuff," he knelt next to a bag and dug through it.

Sam watched the two until they finished ransacking the small camp. He stayed where he was for some time after they were gone. He'd learned a lot of caution wandering around alone. He was beginning to think it might be safe to leave his hiding place when he saw the young girl creep out of the shadow of another building. Sam settled back to watch and see if she was a threat or not. While he watched, the girl approached the body lying on the ground.

"Glenn?" The girl's voice was soft and hesitant.

When there was no response the girl moved in closer to touch the man. She knelt there, softly weeping. Sam watched her for a long time. Longer than was safe. He was getting anxious about the others coming back, or some new threat showing up. He started to leave but a shuddering sob from the girl stopped him. He felt her sadness and wanted to comfort her. His instincts told him it was dangerous but he approached her anyway.

"What?" The girl noticed Sam out of the corner of her eye.

She wiped at her eyes and watched him. He could feel her fear still, and grief when he met her eyes. She was afraid of him. Sam sat down and lowered his head so he was looking up at her. She smiled and reached out to touch his head gingerly. He pressed his head into her palm, glad to finally have some human contact. She leaned forward, rested her forehead against the top of his head and wept softly.

Sam stayed that way until his anxiety got to be too much. Sitting still too long in the open was a sure way to get killed. He moved out from under her, took her sleeve between his teeth and pulled gently before walking off a few feet. She looked at him curiously and wiped her eyes again.

"What is it, boy?"

Sam tilted his head and looked in the direction the other two people went. He heard no sign of them, so gave a low gruff and took a couple steps in the opposite direction.

The girl picked up her pack, which was nearly empty. She took one last look at the man lying in the dirt and bent to kiss his cheek. Sam could tell she wanted to stay with her packmate, but the man was dead. There was no time to grieve. No time to bury the dead or say goodbye. Scavengers would soon pick up the scent, and Sam wanted to be long gone before that. He gave another low gruff and the girl stood to follow him.

The pair walked for hours until the sun rose through the haze on the distant horizon. The girl was stumbling along next to Sam, barely looking up from the broken ground. The heat was already rising and Sam was getting tired himself. He checked the air for the smell of clean water. They would both need it before the heat of the day settled in.

When Sam caught a promising scent, he veered off to investigate. The girl continued to trudge along their original path with her head down. Sam stopped and gave a soft bark to get her attention.

"Hmm?" The girl stopped and looked at Sam. Her eyes were red and wet.

Sam gruffed again and stepped between two broken concrete walls. The girl followed without another word. Sam led her away from the open path to where several large ruins had collapsed. The buildings were once tall but now appeared to have their tops sheared off by unimaginable force. The part that remained had crumbled, parts of its walls fallen to create a mound of stone around the bottom two floors. It was through one of those dark doorways that Sam smelled water, and something else.

He sat down and watched the crumbling building before him. He continued to sniff the air and listen for any sound from the ruin. They needed water and shelter. Whatever water was in there would burn off in the heat of the day. The girl sat down beside him and rested her head on her knees. She was exhausted. They both needed rest.

Sam could wait no longer. They needed to get under cover before the sun came up. He got up and approached the ruins. The girl stayed where she was, head resting on her knees, while he padded silently toward the doorway. He listened carefully for any sound that might indicate that something was alive inside the ruin. Sam stopped within a few feet of the dark doorway. He tested the air again. Whatever was in there smelled wrong.

As Sam was starting to think it might be better to move on, the wind shifted behind them. It was carrying his scent into the building. He turned to run back to the girl but it was too late. Sam lost the scent of what was inside the ruin, but he could hear it stir. The shift in the wind had alerted it to intruders and while Sam could probably get away, he knew the girl would stand no chance.

Sam turned back toward the dark opening. He put himself between whatever was moving inside and the little girl still sitting unaware behind. The creature was coming into view when the wind shifted again. Its smell was stronger and washed over Sam ahead of its attack. And attack it did.

The creature was once feline. That was clear from the smell, but it was twisted and unnatural. Sam had seen other animals that looked, and smelled, wrong. Something in the air or water affected them. More than their bodies, it affected their minds. The animals that were changed acted strangely. They behaved differently than Sam expected. There was a part of him that understood how the world should be and they didn't fit that world anymore. He wondered if he had changed too.

The mutated cat was as big as Sam and covered in patches of wiry hair. Between the patches was cracked and blistered skin shiny from some secretion caused by whatever it had been exposed to. Sam was a large dog, standing nearly as tall as the little girl's shoulder. Sam realized the cat's size made it a serious danger to both of them. Its long, spindly legs ended in paws that were tipped with jagged and broken claws.

The creature's claws dug into the rubble and dirt beneath as it launched itself toward Sam. Sam planted his own wide paws and lowered his head. He realized, almost too late what his enemy's real target was. The monster tried to veer around Sam to reach the vulnerable prey beyond. It probably believed it could carry the child off before Sam could stop it. Sam was faster. He planted his back paws and lunged. He hit the twisted feline hard. It was quick, and turned in time to narrowly avoid Sam's powerful jaws. The two went down in a rolling heap, both clawing for the upper hand in the struggle. The cat twisted and thrashed to keep out of Sam's strong jaws, and its claws were tearing viciously at his hide.

Sam finally rolled his larger bulk over on top of the creature and pinned it to the ground. The mutated beast thrashed wildly under him and managed to keep itself out of his grasp. The feline raked Sam's face, barely missing his eyes. It gave Sam the opening he needed though. He lunged in quick and sank his teeth into his adversary's neck. The cat went into a frenzy when Sam latched on. Its claws raked his stomach and legs attempting to find purchase and win its freedom. Each cut was like a line of fire lancing through Sam's skin. He was losing a lot of blood and the pain threatened his concentration but he latched on tighter and used his thick neck muscles to jerk and shake his enemy.

The feline finally got its claws into Sam's muzzle, searching for his eyes with the razor-sharp weapons. Sam let go and jerked his head back before it could do any serious damage. Even so, Sam could taste blood from his lacerated snout. The cat leaped back and crouched. Sam could hear the girl screaming now and so could his enemy. The emaciated feline was clearly driven by his hunger and trying to decide if it could get past Sam and make off with the softer prey.

Sam shook his head and sneezed blood to clear his muzzle. He watched the cat closely and when the creature made its move, he was ready. The cat leaped, trying to get past him again. Sam charged, jaws wide, and managed to latch onto the thing's neck at the base of its skull. The mutant tried to roll over to claw at Sam's belly again but Sam was prepared for the move. He put both of his large paws down on its back to keep the creature immobile. Then he pulled and jerked, much like he would do when playing tug rope with his family. The cat thrashed and screamed but Sam's weight kept it pinned. Finally, Sam felt a pop, and the mutated feline went still in his jaws.

Sam spat the cat out and wretched. The beast tasted foul, and its blood was worse. The girl was sobbing now and covering her face a few feet away. He limped over to her slowly so as not to frighten her further, and because the pain was excruciating. When he stood in front of her, he licked her fingers. She opened her hands and looked at him, letting out another choking sob at his appearance. She reached out and stroked his bloody muzzle, careful to keep her fingers away from the terrible lacerations. She smoothed his fur while he weakly licked her hand.

"Poor doggie," the girl said. "What do I do now."

Sam stepped back slowly and looked toward the hard-won shelter. The sun was nearly up and he was desperately thirsty. The girl looked that way too and seemed to understand. She stood and walked with him toward the ruined building. Each step closer to the dark doorway was an agony for the canine.

Once inside Sam easily located the water. An old bathtub had been collecting rainwater that fell through a hole in the roof. It smelled clean so he leaned in to drink noisily, making room for the girl to do the same. After they drank their fill Sam found a dark corner where the ground was free of debris and lay down. Before he could fall asleep though, the girl was next to him wiping his fur with something damp. The girl had torn part of her shirt and wet it in the tub. She was gingerly wiping the blood and muck out of the fur around his wounds. He whimpered when she brushed against particularly painful spots but resisted the urge to snap at her.

"I'm sorry, I want to make sure it isn't too bad."

The girl cleaned Sam's wounds for what seemed like hours. She tied a sleeve, torn from her shirt, over a wound on his flank that was still bleeding. Finally, she sat back, exhausted. She closed her eyes and rested her head back against a fallen block. Sam was grateful for her care but he was still in a lot of pain and extremely weak. He climbed into the girl's lap and lay down, as much for his own comfort as hers. She carefully wrapped her arms around him and absently stroked his unmarred neck until they both drifted off.

Sam woke hours later. It was close to dark outside and the girl was still asleep. He got to his feet slowly, feeling the pain lancing through him like fire. He was hungry but in no shape to hunt. There was still clean water in the tub so he drank his fill, leaving some for his companion, and limped to the door facing the broken street. The cat's body was no longer there, probably carried off by scavengers. He sniffed the air but detected nothing. As far as he could tell there was nothing, or no one close.

Turning back to the dark ruin Sam saw the girl already stirring. He sat and waited for her to splash water on her face and take a drink. He wanted to avoid moving any more than he had to. She gathered her few things and walked over to him to scratch between his ears. It made him forget the pain for a minute.

"I'm hungry," she said.

The men that attacked her had taken all the food. She only had her bag, with a few odd articles of clothing inside.

"Come on, boy, there's a place nearby we were going to search."

She walked away from the ruin and away from Sam's original direction of travel. He was originally moving the same direction his family had been before the attack. He was seriously hurt, however, and the girl was alone. Sam spent another moment of indecision but then turned to follow the girl. For the time being they needed each other.

"My name is Susie, not that you can understand me. I just miss talking to Glenn already."

Sam padded along silently of course, but he could tell they were alone for the moment so he let her talk. She seemed more relaxed than the day before, and less vulnerable. Vulnerability got you killed, so Sam was glad for the shift. Nothing she said made any sense to him, but it seemed to help her.

They walked through the ruins of the old city for hours past dark before Susie stopped in front of the one building still mostly standing in the area. It was only a single story, surrounded by tall ruins. One of its neighbors had partially buried the back of it in rubble from collapsed walls.

The front was all open like it had been all glass with metal frames, but that was long gone. Susie stood in the middle of the old street listening. Sam was testing the air like he always did. They were, thankfully, alone except for tiny animals that were no danger to them. Sam may have gone for one of those if he were up for it.

"Let's go see if there's anything left," she said after she was satisfied the building was empty. She waited a moment to see if Sam moved. When he stepped toward the ruin, she felt safe to follow.

Sam sniffed around the place once inside. Food was the last thing he expected to find in the old building, but he checked anyway. He could smell the waste of many rodents and hoped to catch one unaware that he could snatch up without much effort. Susie was on the floor as well, looking under old metal shelves and racks. Sam wondered if she was trying to find a rodent to catch as well.

"Ha!" Susie shouted excitedly.

The sudden noise startled Sam and he limped around some debris to see what had caused it. Susie was on the ground with her arm under a rack. She seemed to be straining to reach something. After a few moments, she smiled gleefully and pulled back her arm to reveal a sealed can of something. The treasure had fallen and rolled under the shelving to remain undiscovered until Susie came along. There was no picture on the can to tell them what it was but they'd soon find out as she sat down to open it with a sharp tool she pulled from her pocket.

"Glenn showed me where to look to find food people couldn't see, or reach," Susie explained.

As soon as her tool pierced the can the aroma of processed food reach Sam's nose. The food was impossible to identify by smell, but his mouth watered in anticipation. It was rare that he got what his family called people food, and it was always a treat. Susie pulled the lid off the can and Sam shifted in barely suppressed excitement. All the pain was forgotten for the moment.

"It's not much," Susie apologized.

She scooped a little of the brownish meat paste with two fingers and started to raise them to her mouth. She stopped and held the food out to Sam. He hesitated. As much as he wanted that bite of food, he still knew his place in the world.

"Go on, you're hurt," Susie said, waving her fingers at him.

Sam carefully took her fingers in his mouth to lick the food from them. Despite his hunger, he resisted the urge to bite down. It tasted like meat but its origin was a mystery. It may not have been real meat at all. He was just grateful that it was edible and standing still. Susie retrieved her fingers to scoop more of the paste for herself. Sam watched patiently while she ate her own mouthful. He shifted from foot to foot again when she pulled her fingers back to dip them into the can again.

"Pretty good isn't it?" She asked with a smile.

Sam gruffed softly and Susie giggled while she scooped more food out for him. They ate like that until the can was empty. They finished the small can in a few minutes but it felt like a long respite for both of them. Susie held out the empty can and she laughed as Sam thrust his entire muzzle into it to get at whatever was left.

"We should go," Susie finally said.

Sam felt it too. They had stayed in the same place longer than they should and they were exposed in the open-front building next to the wide street. They exited the ruin to look up and down the rubble-strewn street. Sam's concern proved valid when a breeze up the street brought the scent of other people with it. Familiar people.

"Seems we may not starve today after all," a man's voice growled from the corner of the building as Sam and Susie exited.

Susie screamed when she saw the men from the attack. Sam's hackles raised and he growled low in his throat. He knew he was in no condition to run from them but maybe Susie could escape if he bought her some time.

Susie did run and the men laughed. One of them tried to get around Sam to go after her but the large dog shifted and bared his teeth. They both turned their focus on him, unsure if they could take him alone without serious injury. They separated, intending to come from both sides at once, but Sam moved first. He lunged at the smaller of the two. The man was caught off guard and the dog clamped down on his forearm before he could get out of the way. Sam's prior injuries were bleeding again and the pain was excruciating, but he held on as the man tried to shake him off. The other man hesitated, unsure what to do. Sam bit down harder, tasting blood in his mouth as the man's efforts to dislodge him caused his teeth to sink deeper and tear at his flesh.

Finally, the man's friend found the nerve to help, and a metal pipe. He struck Sam hard, knocking him free with a yelp. The other man kicked Sam, sending him spinning to land in a heap against some broken stone. The man with the pipe stepped forward to take another swing at Sam when a large stone hit him in the forehead.

Susie found a way to climb onto the roof of the ruined store while the men were focused on Sam. Stones and brick from the nearby building collapse littered the roof with plenty of ammunition and she had become adept at hunting small animals with rocks. She'd seen the man kick Sam and anger lent force to her throw. The man dropped the pipe and clutched at his bleeding forehead while his friend searched for the assailant. He spotted her in time to see the brick coming. It hit him in the face, smashing his nose. Susie screamed her rage at them as she lifted a larger piece of concrete over her head and cast it down. The missile sailed close to the man with the newly broken nose. The two took the opening to stumble away but Susie had plenty of ammunition. She cast another stone, the size of her fist, and hit the pipe-wielder in the back of the head. He fell to his hands and knees. His friend helped him up and they disappeared around a corner to avoid any more flying rocks.

Susie waited, breathing heavily but armed with another brick. She was worried about Sam, who lying so still in the dirt. She wanted to make sure the men were gone before she climbed down. She was too far away to see if Sam was breathing, or maybe moving ever so slightly. Concern for Sam outweighed her worry that the men would return. She climbed down the rubble pile that gave her access to the roof and ran to the fallen dog.

She reached Sam in a rush and fell to her knees next to him. He looked so much smaller curled in a ball in the dirt. She was afraid to touch him so she watched to see if he moved, or breathed. After what seemed like forever Sam's chest fluttered with a shuddering breath.

Susie wanted to cry but there was no time for that. All she could think of was to get him out of the street and somewhere safe. The two men, or something worse, could set upon them at any moment. Looking around she could see no way to move the dog. She could pick him up and carry him, but she knew she'd tire too quickly to make it far.

"My pack," she thought out loud.

Susie pulled her nearly empty pack off, then her coat after a moment's consideration. She opened the pack all the way and laid it on the ground next to Sam. Next, she laid out her coat as flat as she could get it. As carefully as possible Susie slid her hands under Sam and started to slide him onto her coat. He whined sharply and snapped at her but seemed to have trouble moving and missed her arm. She took a deep breath and moved him the rest of the way in one swift motion. Sam whined and whimpered and Susie did cry then. She kept moving, however. She tied the sleeves of her coat together and tucked its folds around Sam so that only his head stuck out. She wanted to bundle him up to prevent himself from making his injuries worse. He'd be warm and cushioned as much as possible.

Once he was bundled up tight Susie slid Sam into her pack and zipped it up so his head stuck up over the edge of the opening. He only whimpered slightly, and was breathing heavily when she was done. She put her arms through the straps of the pack and cinched them tight before trying to stand. He was heavier than anything she had ever carried but she was able to get to her feet using the rubble pile. Sam struggled a moment against the restraint but settled down with his head on her shoulder, breathing weakly in her ear.

They walked like that for the rest of the night, finding a basement to shelter in for the day. Sam was still asleep so Susie left him in his bundle. She found a little water but wanted to let Sam sleep so she saved it for the next night. When she woke up, she was able to get Sam to weakly lap at a small bowl of water. She wished she had some food but she found nothing before they had to find shelter. Her shoulders and back hurt like they never had before. It was difficult hoisting Sam up onto her back but she managed it after a couple tries.

They traveled for two nights, resting in small shelters for the days between. Susie was able to find food but they would need more. She was exhausted and her muscles ached. By the beginning of the third night she could barely get herself to her feet. The dog was so still and she could barely feel his ragged breath against the back of her neck. She knew she would need to find food and water that night or he would probably die.

Once on her feet, she trudged on in the same direction they'd been heading before the second attack. She had no destination in mind so figured that direction was as good as any other. She walked with her head down and each tired step scattered dust and stones in her path. If a predator spotted them, she knew they would be easy prey.

She made it a few hours before falling the first time. She bashed her knees on the stones and scraped the skin from her palms. Sam was so still and she considered taking off the pack. Every muscle in her body screamed at her to lose the extra weight and go on alone. Instead, she took a deep breath and struggled to her feet again.

She only made it another few yards before crashing to the broken pavement again. This time she was overcome with tears. It was frustration, more than the pain, that got the better of her. She'd failed Sam and herself. They were both likely to die in the dust and there was nothing she could do about it. She tried to push herself to her feet, but her body failed to cooperate. She rested her head in the dirt for a moment. It was the opening the darkness was waiting for to drag her below the waves of consciousness.

Sometime later Sam heard voices he recognized, then he smelled familiar scents. Susie was lying still under him. He had no concept of how long they had been lying in the road, or how long it had been since he was wounded by the men. He was unable to move, and the pain was like a dull ache waiting to pounce at any moment. The voices were getting closer and Sam was getting anxious.

"What's this?" A man's voice asked nearby.

Sam whined and opened his eyes.

"Sam?" A woman's voice this time.

Sam's tail twitched as much as it could. Memories of the last time he saw his family flooded back. The attack on the bridge, gunshots, and Sam falling into the water to be washed downstream played through his mind. Their pack was smaller though. Sam could smell most of his family, but the boy and the older man were missing.

"She's still breathing too," the woman called Mom said.

She was close. Sam smelled woodsmoke and recently cooked meat. She had washed her hair with the soap she cherished and used whenever it rained. She smelled like home. Then the man called Dad was close and Sam felt the reassuring presence of their pack leader. He waited for the boy, Son, to show up but somehow, Sam knew he wouldn't. Their pack had changed, but Sam was home. Susie had brought them both home.

Wastelander

The world spun around Dez as he tried to regain his senses. Blood caked in his right eye and blocked his vision, his shield arm was limp and useless, and he was distinctly aware of his enemy hovering over him. He could hear the clink of metal as his opponent raised a weapon over his head. Dez wondered what he was waiting for, was he savoring his victory, or was fate having its final laugh, allowing Dez time to realize how much he would lose today? The search for his sister would be over. The vengeance for his murdered parents would be left unfulfilled.

Dez could almost feel the cold steel of his enemy's sword above his neck. No! The word resounded in his head. He was unsure if he shouted it aloud or if it was all in his mind.

He refused to go out on his knees like an animal. His grip tightened on the metal shaft of his axe, and his boots slipped on the gravel as he fought to rise. He could hear his enemy chuckle at his attempt. His boots found purchase, but instead of standing up he lurched forward into his enemy's legs. With a cry of surprise, the armored man hit the ground; his legs tangled with Dez's arms. The pain in Dez's left arm was excruciating as the other kicked and fought to free himself.

Dez managed to get to his feet before his enemy did, and he kicked the man in the mouth with his steel-capped boot. Blood and teeth flew as the armored man fell to the ground clutching his sundered face. Dez bent to retrieve his axe from the ground before confronting his fallen enemy. He kicked away the man's sword and placed his boot on his enemy's steel-encased chest. He looked down on the armored man with his clear gray eyes, no sign of emotion on his square face. He was broader than the man on the ground, with large muscles in his shoulders and chest from swinging his axe. Dez wore a sleeveless suit of hardened leather armor which hung down to his knees. His legs were bare between the kirtle of his armor and his leather boots which stopped right below his knees.

"Where is Pontius?" Dez asked in a gravelly whisper. The man turned his head and spat out blood, but remained silent. Dez brought his axe down swiftly on the man's arm, taking it off at the elbow.

"Where is Pontius?" Dez asked again when the man's screams quieted into grunts and gasps.

"If I tell you, you will kill me anyway, and if you don't Pontius will," the man gasped.

"Tell me, and your death will be quick; don't and you die by inches," Dez said calmly, raising his axe again.

The man looked into Dez's eyes, pleading for mercy, but there was none to be found there. Finally, he said, "His citadel is three days south of here, in the mountains above the Wild River. There is a cleft in the cliff face, at a ford. You can't miss it. Follow the canyon right to his stronghold. You will never make it though, he has soldiers guarding all approaches to the pass," this last was said to Dez's back. Dez retrieved his shield and his enemy's sword.

"Hey, you can't leave me out here. You said you would kill me."

"I lied," Dez called back as the fallen man tried to get up. The pain was too much for him and he fell back retching. Dez strapped his shield and new sword onto the harness behind his mount's saddle and returned his axe to the carrier on his back.

"You can't just leave me here, the scavengers will have me," the man begged, clutching his bleeding stump, trying to staunch the flow of blood.

"Then I suggest you find a deep hole and hide in it," Dez said. He turned his mount's horned head east without giving the man another thought. He was so close, but he knew he would die of his injuries before making it to Pontius's stronghold. The Tower was a day and a half ride east, and the healers there would tend his wounds. The healers would help anyone that came to their doorstep as long as the patient behaved while in the Tower. A force of warriors, known simply as paladins, lived at the Tower to ensure that peace was kept, and the healers, who were pacifists, were protected.

"Let's go Vroc," Dez said softly, patting his mount's thick neck. The beast was a rarity on Theron called a saark. It was a savage equine creature and hard to break, making them undesirable to most. Once broken, though, a saark was a ferociously loyal mount. Saarks were heavily muscled animals with four sharp hooves and equally sharp teeth. They had thick curved horns that burst from the back of their skulls and pointed toward their noses. Their coats were shaggy with a long mane and hair that covered their hooves. Vroc had saved Dez's life many times and had proven himself a savage companion in combat. Despite the animal's ability to fight, he chose the worst times to test Dez and, like this most recent encounter, to stay out of a fight. Even when they are broken, a saark would abandon weak masters.

* * *

"Dez?"

"No!"

"Dez, wake up, it's only a dream," a woman's voice said in the dark.

Dez rose through the darkness to find himself in a clean and quiet room. He took in his surroundings as the waking world slowly came back to him. He was in a bed, but where? The Tower, he was in the Tower of the Healers. One of those healers was sitting on the edge of his bed, and there was a strange weightlessness to his left arm. There was some pain, mostly throbbing in his arm and head.

"Kara?" Dez whispered. He avoided looking at his shield arm, as if he could ignore the reality of recent events.

"Dez, I'm sorry. There was too much damage," Kara explained as Dez rolled over, away from her. "You barely made it here, and if your beast wasn't so smart you would have died out there. He brought you in, unconscious and feverish, but you reached us in time."

Dez only heard "I'm sorry." He was in shock and denial about what happened to him. How could he avenge his parents, and save his sister? How would he protect himself with only one arm? His shield arm would be useless in combat, but he had to go on. She was counting on him.

Dez rolled onto his back and lifted what remained of his left arm. Where most of his forearm and hand should have been there was a bandage. Seeing the bandage gave him an idea.

"Kara, bring the blacksmith up here," Dez said calmly.

* * *

"Dez, you need a few more days of rest," Kara said, looking down at his left arm. The limb was now capped by a steel mechanism complete with strange slots and hooks.

"You have my thanks, Kara, for all you and the sisters have done, but I am too close. I know where he is, and my sister is waiting," Dez said, tightening the straps on Vroc's harness. He used a hook on his left arm to hold a buckle while his free hand cinched it. The blacksmith had made quick work of Dez's idea to return some functionality to the ruined arm. The process had been painful but they were both happy with the results. With a slight modification to his shield, the warrior could now attach that to his left arm quickly.

"Be careful out there Dez," Kara put a hand on his muscular shoulder. Dez turned and smiled, briefly touching her cheek with a thick, calloused finger. She closed her eyes for a heartbeat and stepped away. Dez could feel paladins in the courtyard take a step toward him. He met the dark look of one over Kara's shoulder. With a mock salute to that paladin, Dez mounted Vroc and turned his head toward the gate.

Kara watched Dez ride Vroc out of the courtyard of the Tower and thought back on how many times she had done that in the past. She met Dez years ago when he was brought to the Tower as a child. Raiders killed his parents, took his sister, and left him bloody and near death. She was in training then, still a girl herself, and had helped nurse the boy back to health. That created a bond stronger than either had ever known but it was a bittersweet relationship. Kara's vows kept them apart. Even if she were free, though, he was too obsessed with his search to give himself to her.

Dez came to the Tower many times over the years, and against the Head Mother's advice, Kara made sure she was the one to treat him every time. The sisters knew what was going on, and they pitied her for how it would end. It was not uncommon for a patient to fall in love with one of the sisters, but the healers usually took steps to avoid the it.

*   *   *

Dez looked back to see the top of the Tower slipping below the horizon. It was an unusual structure rising out of the wasted landscape around it. People who seemed to know more about the world said that the tall, angular building was the ruin of some ancient civilization and that the sisters had occupied it since the Cleansing. Dez lived in the present and left the dusty and useless histories to other men. All he knew for sure was no one could have built it after the world ended. The sisters lived a solitary life in the Tower with only the paladins for company. The nearest settlement was a day west by horse.

The Tower was one bright spot in a wasteland full of raiders, scavengers, and all kinds of other dangers. The paladins and the heavy wall kept the sisters safe from all of that, and the nearby settlement kept them supplied with food and other goods in exchange for regular visits from the sisters. Their skills were a mystery and a fiercely protected secret.

As far as anyone knew they were the only ones with real healing skills, and this was a danger all its own. A captured healer sold for a king's ransom on the slave market. The sisters themselves charged nothing for their services, but patients frequently made donations before they left the Tower.

Dez turned his mind back to the task at hand. It was unwise to let one's mind wander for too long while traveling the Wasteland. He had three or four days of travel ahead of him barring any unexpected delays. Counting on a smooth ride would be pointless, however.

Traveling the Waste was an exercise in determination and preparedness. Along with all the natural dangers, rock falls, pits, corrosive pools, and sandstorms, travelers had to worry about vicious beasts and violent raiders. The scavengers were the worst. A hairless canine beast, they were nearly as tall as a man at the shoulders. They traveled in packs, hunting the Waste for anything edible whether it was alive or rotting. If you avoided the scavenger packs then you had to be on the lookout for raiders, bands of people that lived by taking from others. The raiders also tended to move in packs, but many times they were less intelligent than scavengers.

The sun beat down on Dez as he guided Vroc through the rocky landscape toward the mountains in the distance. He was making good time, but that was expected. Raiders and scavengers gave the Tower a wide berth due to the paladin patrols. He would need to find shelter for the night though. A walled settlement would be perfect, but Dez would settle for a cave in a hillside, whatever he could find that he could defend easily.

The day wore on as Dez continued south. He could feel the sweat pouring down his body under the protection of his leather armor. He ate a lunch of dried meat at midday and washed it down with small sips of the clean water the sisters packed for him. Clean water was hard to find in the Waste, so he would have to make it last. Vroc would be able to travel the rest of the day before he needed water or rest. He saw only one other group of people, a paladin patrol. They were some distance away when they saw him, but they continued on their way. A lone traveler moving away from the Tower posed no threat, so they left him alone.

About an hour before sundown Dez found a shelter that he decided would have to do. An abandoned hovel was built against a hillside surrounded by the remains of a failed attempt at a garden. The Waste was generally inhospitable, but a few hardy people managed to squeeze a living out of the land. No such luck at this farm. It looked deserted, but Dez was taking no chances. He moved Vroc forward slowly, staying alert for any signs of danger. The hut remained quiet and showed no signs of life as Vroc picked his way through the detritus of the rotting garden.

When approached to the hovel it appeared to be deserted and surprisingly secure. It had four walls, a roof, and no windows. It was more luxury than Dez could expect on the Waste. The door was even serviceable after he repaired it, something that was difficult with one arm but Dez adapted and found ways to use his metal-capped stump. After their safety was seen to, Dez brought Vroc inside and gave him some food and water. Saarks preferred meat but could eat almost anything, which was a great benefit considering the scarcity of food on the Waste. Unlike a horse, Vroc required no special care or grooming. Dez did keep his coat free of burs and other irritants that the beast was unable to reach himself. Once these tasks were done the two settled down for the night. Vroc lay down against the door, and Dez sat with his back against the saark holding his axe across his knees.

The two spent a cold, restless night in the relative safety of the one-room hut. The Wasteland was extraordinarily hot during the day, but at night the temperature dropped dramatically. It was also the time that the scavenger packs came out of their dens to hunt. Their calls, an eerie barking howl, came close at times, but never close enough to be a concern. Their calls sounded like people screaming in the distance, interrupted by yelps and sharp barking grunts. Inexperienced travelers often mistook the sounds for people being attacked by dogs of some kind. As usual, when Dez managed to sleep his dreams were the same. Flashes of his sister and parents, fire, blood, and pain. He found that he welcomed the dreams. As painful as they were, they fueled his desire for revenge.

*　　　*　　　*

Vroc nudged Dez awake when sunlight began to filter through the cracks in the walls of their shelter. Dez got up and stretched, relieved himself outside, and then shared a meager breakfast with Vroc. While they ate Dez took a large skin out of one of the packs on Vroc's saddle along with a piece of charred wood. Finding his reference points he marked the hut about a day south of the Tower. The Tower itself occupied the center of his crude map. Other marks indicated settlements, caves, scavenger dens, raider camps, and safe places to stay the night. Along with his weapons, the map was one of his most prized possessions, and he took great care with it. After he was satisfied with his work Dez folded the map and replaced it in the saddlebag.

    "Let's go Vroc," Dez pushed the saark's head away from the pouch of dried meat, "It's already starting to get hot."

    Dez mounted and turned Vroc's head to the south. There was a settlement in that direction, but they would have to make good time to reach it before dark. He pushed Vroc into a quick trot. A saark was slower than a horse but it made up for it in endurance. The beast would be able to keep up this pace almost all day without rest.

    Traveling through the day was much like any other on the Waste, hot, dry, and solitary. Few people lived on the blasted desert, and fewer still were willing to travel outside their settlements. People tended to band together for protection and survival. Some banded together to form communities, and some banded together to feed off the hard work of others. It was hard work to live on the Waste except for relics of the ancients, but many chose it because of the freedom. Life outside the region was usually one of servitude to some tyrannical warlord or greedy landowner. Relic hunters were often hired to find the artifacts that were used to power many of the conveniences outlanders valued. It was a dangerous job and Wastelanders did not usually take kindly to the theft or export of those artifacts.

Dez liked the solitude. Encountering other people meant always having to decide if they were a threat. The company of others was something he tended to avoid. He could count, on one hand, the ones in his life he would carry on a conversation with. One of them was a saark. Maybe that would all change once he killed Pontius and got his sister back, but he doubted it.

His musings were cut short when Vroc snorted and sidestepped. Dez looked around, searching the nearby rocks and then the horizon. He took note of the lowering sun but saw no visible danger that could have alerted the saark. He looked down at the beast and noticed the flared nostrils, it was something on the wind then. Smoke or scavengers would cause that kind of reaction, but there was no smoke in sight. They must be close to a den of sleeping scavengers.

Dez reigned in the saark and concentrated. He felt the wind blowing lightly from the south. Great, he thought, the den was somewhere between them and the settlement. Dez kicked Vroc into a fast trot again, but the beast needed no coaxing. Dez scanned the darkening landscape, looking for signs of either the scavengers or the settlement. Most people at this point would give in to hope. Hope that they had time to get away, or that they could evade the scavengers. Dez put no stock in hope. He preferred to prepare for the worst, and if the worst was what happened then it was no more than what he expected.

The final hour or so of sunlight was bathing the desert in a red-orange fire when Dez finally spotted the walls of the settlement on the horizon. He was slightly off course and behind schedule, so he turned Vroc to head to the southwest and tried to coax more speed out of the saark. While they moved he reached back with his good hand and unbuckled his shield from its place behind his saddle. Steadying his other arm, he fixed the metal clasps on the back of the round shield into the sockets on the metal cap. The wound was still painful, and the added weight caused him to grimace. The pain made him angry, at himself and the man who caused it. It was an inconvenience which could slow him down. He took the reins back in his free hand and scanned the horizon again. Damn, he thought, we are cutting this close. The scavengers would come out of their den before he could get to the safety of the settlement's walls.

Scavengers were night hunters due to their poor eyesight. Their sense of smell and hearing more than made up for it, giving them an advantage over their prey at night. Encountering them during the day was still dangerous. Many a wanderer had walked too close to, or stumbled right into, one of their dens. It never ended well.

It was when he was close and starting to see the figures of guards on the walls that the first of the scavengers emerge from the den. The last rays of the sun showed the large beast stretching and pulling itself out of the ground. It rose slowly, stretching out the kinks developed from sleeping curled up in a small hole in the ground. The creature was huge, probably the biggest Dez had ever seen. Its hairless body was all muscles and tendons standing out on its wiry frame. It shook itself and then sniffed the air. At least the wind was in their favor, Dez thought. The rest would be in the den still, waiting for this alpha to make sure it was safe. There could be any number of beasts in this pack. They were between him and the settlement so waiting for them to emerge was out of the question.

Dez kicked Vroc for more speed. Normally the saark would balk at such reckless run. A pack of scavengers, however, was one of the few things on the Waste that could take down a saark, so Vroc was willing to make an exception. The horned beast put his head down and charged the scavenger, who was only then becoming aware of the danger. The canine raised its head and rotated its large ears, trying to pinpoint the sound. By the time the creature turned its head in their direction, it was too late. Vroc hit the scavenger like a battering ram, so hard that Dez heard bones crack and a great whoosh of air escape the creature's body. The heavier saark barely slowed and barreled past, making best speed for the settlement ahead.

The scavenger scrambled to its feet, calling out in its yelping bark. Several of the hairless beasts burst out of their subterranean shelter and identified the sound of the fleeing Vroc. Two of the smaller scavengers sprinted ahead of their peers and started gaining on the saark and his passenger. Dez looked back and saw the oncoming danger in the fading light of day. That was how the pack hunted: the smallest and fastest chasing down the prey to slow it and the larger ones going in for the final kill. Dez drew his axe from its carrier and leaned down low on Vroc's neck so as to offer as little wind resistance as possible.

Vroc snorted and huffed as his energy ebbed. Dez knew they were too slow, and their flight was going to turn into a running fight. He pulled back slightly on the saark's reigns to slow him down, giving them a better chance to avoid a mishap that could end it all. Dez looped the reins loosely around a saddle hook and lowered the axe so he gripped it lightly by the end of the haft. He watched their shadows on the ground to his left, but otherwise, he let it appear that he was unaware of the scavenger's proximity. Scavengers were intelligent, but he figured they would still fall for the ruse.

The scavengers played along as Dez thought they might. Thinking that their prey was fleeing in a blind panic the predators recklessly charged in for the kill. Dez watched the shadows as one beast leaped for him and the other raced ahead to lunge for Vroc's neck. When the first was in the air he ducked under it and brought his axe around, aiming for the beast still on the ground. He swung the axe in a circular motion, building up tremendous force in the head of the weapon. The blade finished its rotation as he leaned low in the saddle, cleaving deeply into the scavenger's back. Muscle and bone gave way under the heavy blade, and the beast let out a startled yelp as its legs failed. It tumbled in the dirt and was left behind.

The scavenger that had leaped over Dez landed hard and scrambled to gain its feet. The beast turned but was caught under the churning hooves of the saark. By some devilish miracle, the monster survived and gave chase as soon as Vroc passed over. Dez looked back and saw the surviving scavenger with the rest of the pack close behind. He looked again at the walls of the settlement he was approaching.

"We just might make this," Dez patted Vroc's neck and prepared to defend them from the nearest scavenger. The beast caught up with them easily. It was clawing frantically at Vroc's flanks, trying to get a hold of something to drag them down.

Dez turned and drove the rim of his shield into the scavenger's face. The beast yelped but managed to dig his claws into Dez's leg. The claws were sharp and easily cut through his leather kirtle and found purchase on the bone in his thigh. Dez gritted his teeth against the pain and fended off the snapping jaws of the predator with his shield. Knowing that time was of the essence he dropped his axe, which was useless this close, and drew a long knife from his boot. The beast pulled up and snapped again, and this time Dez let it past his shield. He drove his knife into the roof of the monster's open mouth, cutting his hand open on the sharp teeth in the process. The scavenger yelped, lost its grip on Dez, and fell into the dirt pawing frantically at the blade in its face.

Dez rode within sight of the settlement's defenders and saw the archers leveling bows in his direction. He thrust his hands out to show he was unarmed and shouted as loudly as he could, "Scavengers behind!"

The archers wasted no time, adjusting their aim slightly and fired arrows over Dez's head. He heard some of the missiles connect and others clatter on the hard-pack. He heard the yelps and cries behind him, but he kept his eyes forward. He rode hard for the gates that were slowly opening to let him and the saark pass. The archers stopped firing so he had to assume the scavengers were driven off. Dez rode through the gate, passing through a small group of guards, and put his hands out to the side again. Settlers on the Waste took no chances, especially at night.

"Gods Dez, you sure know how to make an entrance," a guard said as the gates were being closed, "And what in the hells happened to your arm?"

"Thelin?" Dez asked, trying to see the guard's face, but his helm and the darkness were obscuring his face.

"Yah, it's me," Thelin said.

"They finally rope you into the militia?" Dez asked with a smile, but his face turned into a grimace as pain shot up his leg.

"Let's get you looked at before you die on me," Thelin reached for Vroc's reins. The saark growled and tried to bite the guard, but the man was faster and slapped the beast hard on the nose, "Mind your manners you old mule."

Thelin led them to the old woman who passed as the settlement's healer. The woman had a small house near the edge of town that was indistinguishable from the other ramshackle dwellings. She answered the door soon after Thelin's knock, long used to being roused for emergencies after dark. She took Dez inside to check him over. He looked around the wise woman's home and noted the stark contrast between and the Healer's Tower. Her house was meticulously clean, but that's where any similarity ended. Scattered about were pieces and parts of animals, some whole, and in various types of preservation. Dried herbs and other plants hung from rafters. Between it all the tools of the medicine woman's trade were scattered about. Under it all, not a speci of dust or spot of grime was to be found. Outside, Thelin cleaned some scratches and cuts that Vroc had picked up in the fight. The guard had to smack the animal two more times to remind him of his place.

The old woman vigorously cleaned the wound in Dez's leg while he gripped the arms of a chair. After taking a good look at it she determined he would heal without help from one of the Sisters of the Tower. She smeared it with a pungent paste from a large crock and bound it tightly with some cloth. Once his leg was patched, she turned her attention to his good hand. The wounds were gruesome, but not life-threatening so she applied more paste and wrapping. Her ministrations were rough, but she was skilled. She assured Dez that he would be able to put all his weight on the leg in no time. Dez thanked the woman and met Thelin outside.

The guard smiled when Dez limped out of the healer's home, "She patch you up?"

Dez nodded and took Vroc's reins. He looked the saark over and patted the beast's muzzle, "Thanks for this, Thelin. That inn still over at the east gate?"

"Yes, it's still there," Thelin replied.

"Join me for a drink?" Dez asked.

"Can't. I have to get back to my post, but I'll look you up for breakfast when my shift is over," Thelin replied. Dez nodded and turned Vroc toward the east gate. Thelin chuckled as he watched the warrior limp away. Always a man of few words, he thought.

*   *   *

When Dez reached the inn, he paid for stable space for Vroc and got the saark settled down for the night. Thankfully only two other mounts were on one end of the stables. The animals were a small breed of pack mule used by merchants. They were stubborn and temperamental but could walk miles under a heavy load without stopping. They cast a wary eye at the saark as Dez led Vroc to the unoccupied end of the building. After he rechecked the saark's wounds and left him some of their dried meat, Dez cuffed the saark's snout and told him to leave the mules alone. He then went inside to see about his own dinner and lodging.

Dez ate in solitude and then went to the common room to sleep. The accommodations were as mediocre as the stew had been. They both got the job done, and it was more than he was used to on a daily basis. Luke warm stew and a dry roof was a luxury compared to life outside the walls of the town. He was pleased to see the blanket was clean, and the cot seemed to be free of vermin. Dez dropped his pack, shield, and the sword he had picked up, into the footlocker at the end of the cot. He locked it with the key that was in the lock and looped the key around his neck by its lanyard. With that done he lay down and settled in for another restless night of horrible dreams and sleepless hours.

*   *   *

Dez lay awake for over an hour and suspected that it was close to dawn. When he saw the sky start to lighten through the grimy window he sighed and slowly got to his feet, testing his weight on the injured leg. It was still sore and tender enough to cause a limp, but he could walk on it. He retrieved his gear and went downstairs to see if he could get some breakfast. When he got down to the taproom, he saw Thelin at a table with a plate of steaming food in front of him and a large sack sitting on the table next to Dez's axe. Thelin smiled and waved him over. Dez joined him and called to the innkeeper for some food.

"You're here early," Dez said.

"Shift ended an hour ago," Thelin poked the bag, "I requisitioned some supplies for you. Your saddlebags looked a bit light. One of the men brought in your weapon when it was light enough to see."

"Thanks, but won't someone miss the food?" Dez nodded at the innkeeper as he set a plate in front of the warrior.

"Nah, it's nothing expensive, just some basics."

Dez nodded. Both men ate in silence for a time. When they were finished Thelin sat back while Dez inspected the contents of the sack.

"What brings you out this way?" Thelin asked.

"I finally know where he is," Dez said without looking up.

"You found someone stupid enough to tell you where Pontius holes up?" Thelin looked surprised.

Dez nodded, "Couple days ago, got a raider to talk. Not before he did this, though." Dez held up his metal-capped arm.

"I know you don't want to hear this Dez, but going after that maniac is dangerous," Thelin said.

"I am too close now, and I will make that monster pay for what he did."

Dez noticed the only other patron in the common room that morning seemed to be taking more than a passing interest in their conversation. Dez eyed the man until the stranger went back to his breakfast.

Dez and Thelin sat quietly while Dez repacked the supplies and returned his axe to its carrier. Thelin knew there was nothing he could say to change his friend's mind, so he gave what support he could by keeping his mouth shut. Thelin followed Dez out to the stables and helped him saddle and harness Vroc. Dez stowed the supplies in the saddlebags and pulled out his map to check the area south of the settlement. He had no markings on that area of the map yet.

"A cave, in the hills south of here. A large boulder that looks like a face marks the opening," Thelin supplied, "You should be able to reach it before dark."

Dez nodded and folded the map away, "Thanks again, Thelin. When I get my sister back I will find some way to return the favor."

"Just come back in one piece," Thelin looked at his arm, "Mostly," he finished with a smile.

Dez smiled and clapped his friend on the shoulder before mounting Vroc. Thelin watched him ride toward the south gate and saluted in farewell. He wondered if he would ever see his friend again.

Dez exited the south gate and put himself on alert again. He took mental stock of his supplies: his axe, sword, one knife in his other boot, and enough food and water to get to Pontius' stronghold and back as long as he was frugal. Satisfied with that he turned his mind to the landscape around him. With only two days to his goal, Dez was careful to prevent some accident on the Waste from stopping him.

Later in the day Dez did, in fact, find the cave that Thelin had mentioned with plenty of time to make sure it was unoccupied and defensible before sunset. He shared some food and water with Vroc, and they got settled in for the night. The saark lay down with his back to the opening, as a windbreak, and Dez sat back against him in their usual fashion. And as usual, he spent the dark hours fighting the daemons in his mind.

*   *   *

The morning sun greeted the Waste with another day of dry, baking heat. Dez had been awake for almost an hour, so he was ready to leave as soon as the sun was up. He was so anxious to head into the mountains and find Pontius' hideout, that he nearly forgot breakfast. Vroc remembered though, and the saark set his hooves and refused to move until he had food and water.

Once breakfast was settled the two got back on the road. The cave they stayed in was at the base of a mountain range that defined the southern border of the Wasteland. Separating the desert from those mountains was the Wild River, so named for the miles of rapids and white water, and its wide fast current. The river came down out of the range somewhere to the east and flowed through the hills and canyons until it emptied into the sea several weeks travel west, outside the Wasteland. It was the only water source in the Wasteland that continuously flowed, but it shirted the edge of the barren land so provided little relief to the desert. Some small settlements sprung up along its course but the river drew every predator and raider in the area, making it a more dangerous place than anywhere else. Dez and Vroc came upon this daunting obstacle about midday.

Dez was not as concerned about crossing the river as he was about the high cliffs on the other side. He located the cut in the cliff face and the ford that Pontius' man had described, and he could see why Pontius had built his stronghold up there. Those cliffs would give defenders a decisive advantage and turn the cut into a death trap. That was foremost in his mind as he scanned the cliffs for any signs of life. The heights looked clear, and even if there was someone up there Dez knew he had little choice. His sister was being held in a stronghold somewhere in those mountains, through that cut.

Dez guided Vroc into the river and the saark carefully picked his way across the ford. The current was strong, but so was Vroc. When they reached the middle, the frigid water was lapping at the rider's knees. It was the perfect spot for an ambush, and Dez knew it. So did the raiders who were hiding among the rocks above. They rose from their hiding places and rained arrows down on Dez and his mount. Many of the shafts zipped into the water and were washed away, but three found their mark.

Two of the missiles hit Vroc in his flank, and the third slammed high into Dez's shoulder, knocking him from the saddle. The current of the river swept them both downstream.

Dez felt a stab of regret as he struggled, with one good arm, to keep his head above water. It made him angry that he was going to end up drowned in a river on the very doorstep of the one he had been looking to kill for years. The current pulled him down several times, and the water choked him. The cold was numbing his entire body, and he was preparing himself for the reality that his mission was over. Those thoughts turned into confused panic as he felt himself become tangled in something in the river, and then forcibly pulled across the rocks and out of the water. He sputtered and coughed, rolling over on his side, and caught a glimpse of several pairs of legs surrounding him. They gave him no time to recover before they beat him into unconsciousness.

*   *   *

Dez awoke in complete darkness. He had trouble opening his eyes. One side of his face felt overly large, and his eye was swollen shut. The other was sealed with something sticky, probably blood. He was tied to something hard and cold, the bonds cutting painfully into his skin. His head throbbed with pain and with the sound of many people around him.

"He's awake boss," called a voice near him.

"About time. Clean out his eye so he can see me," was the response.

A rough, wet cloth was pressed painfully in Dez's eye and used to wipe away the dried blood. Thick fingers pried his eyelids open, and the foul breath of the ugly man that looked into his face gagged him. The man stepped away and another took his place. The man's face was the same one Dez saw in his nightmares, smiling and wreathed in fire.

"So this is the mysterious Wastelander that's been looking for me?" Pontius asked no one in particular as he looked Dez up and down.

"Looks like you've seen better days my friend. You didn't expect to get in here without my notice, did you? I have eyes everywhere"

Dez thought back to the tavern, and the stranger that had shown so much interest in him. He worked his swollen mouth to respond but his throat was too raw and dry. He had plenty of words for the man, but his voice failed him.

"Get this boy some water. He has something to say," Pontius yelled over his shoulder. Several men scrambled to comply. One finally brought a cup to Dez's mouth.

Dez worked his mouth again and tried to speak, but only a rasping cough escaped. Pontius leaned closer to him.

"Sister...going to," Dez swallowed hard, trying to clear his throat, "Kill you," he finished weakly.

Pontius laughed and turned to the people standing around. Dez could now see that he was in a large dining hall full of people. He looked around, but his sister was nowhere to be seen.

"This scamp says he's going to kill me," Pontius shouted.

The assembly laughed as one, whooping and hollering their amusement, all except one. A young girl maybe a few years younger than Dez stood near the back wall. She thought she recognized Dez though and melted into the shadows hoping to remain unnoticed. Pontius looked back at Dez, his face no longer wearing a mask of amusement.

"I think it's time to make another example of one of you Wasteland rats. I can't have any of you thinking you can just come in here and violate my privacy," Pontius punched Dez in the gut, knocking the wind out of him. The raider leaned in close and said softly, "I am going to take my time with you. It's going to be fun… for one of us at least."

Dez's vision swam as Pontius walked away. The damage to his face made breathing difficult, and the pain was making him light-headed. He tried to remain alert, but his body refused to obey. Dez lost the battle and slipped into dark unconsciousness.

*   *   *

"Dez?"

He was dreaming again, but there was no fire this time, only darkness. His sister's voice was calling to him. He thought it was her voice. It sounded deeper though, older maybe, and full of sadness. She touched his face in the darkness, and the pain jerked him back to reality. Dez opened his eye and looked into a face that might be his sister's, under all the dirt and grime. The dining hall was dark and empty behind her.

"Sarah?" Dez asked.

She smiled and pressed her hand to his mouth, signaling silence, "I knew it was you, big brother, but I thought you were dead all these years. What are you doing here?"

"I came to get you and to kill Pontius," he said quietly.

"By yourself? Are you out of your mind, Dez?" She asked quietly. He tried to smile at her, but the pain and swelling turned it into a snarl. "Come on, I have to get you out of here tonight. Pontius will kill you."

"I won't leave without his head," he said as Sarah started to untie him. She stopped, looked closely at him, and shook her head.

"You'll never get close to him. He has six of his most loyal men guard his sleep. Only four watch the gate. We have to leave now, or he will kill both of us," she finally got him freed from the wall.

"There you are, Sarah. What are you doing there?"

"Pontius," Sarah turned with a gasp. Dez stepped forward, pushing his sister behind him. Pontius was alone and unarmed, dressed only in a robe. He took in the scene before him, and a smile of understanding dawned on his face.

"Now I understand why you would be stupid enough to come here alone. I didn't know what you meant before when you said sister, but now I see that I am looking at her," the raider said, "You are weak, boy, injured and out of your league, but I like your spirit so I'll make this quick. I realize I don't need to torture you. You will go to the hells knowing that I still have her."

Dez charged, roaring like an enraged bull, and slammed his shoulder into Pontius' midsection. He wrapped his arms around the man to lift him off the ground. Pontius brought one elbow down on Dez's injured shoulder. Dez grunted, and both men tumbled to the floor amid the stools around the large central table.

Pontius was the first on his feet, but Dez swung his metal-capped forearm and connected with the side of the older man's knee. The bone cracked, and the raider collapsed to the floor again. Dez grabbed the man's ankle and got to his knees above Pontius. Dez raised his arm again to bring the steel cap down on the raider's head, but Pontius put his foot against Dez's chest and pushed him back. The raider rolled, got to his feet, and started limping for the doors.

Dez was close behind and tackled Pontius to the floor. The men struggled for a few seconds, but the raider finally got the leverage he needed and pinned Dez to the floor. He clamped a large hand down on Dez's throat and pinned the Wastelander's body with his knees. Pontius laughed and looked up to call out to his guards, but his shout was cut off when a stool hit him in the back of the head and knocked him aside. When Dez climbed to his feet he saw Sarah standing over the raider with a stool over her head. The look on her face spoke volumes and brought a chill to her brother's spine. With a wrenching sob, she brought the stool down on his head again and then one last time before Dez could stop her and take the stool out of her hands. With another soft cry, she turned into his arms. Dez held her for a minute, looking down at Pontius' corpse. Finally, he held her out by her shoulders and gave her a light shake.

"Sarah, we have to move. His guards will come looking for him soon," Dez said firmly. She looked up and got control of herself.

"I'm fine. Let's go," she said, taking him by the hand and leading him out of the hall.

* * *

Getting out of the stronghold was easier than Dez expected. Pontius' men were undisciplined, especially when it came to something as boring as guard duty. When they had entered the courtyard Dez wanted to steal horses, but Sarah convinced him that it would take too long to saddle and harness them. Reaching the gate they found two of the guards asleep and the other two giving their attention to a game of dice. They made quick work of the guards and fled through the gates.

The two moved as fast as Dez's wounds would allow. He figured that once the raiders found Pontius they would be too busy fighting over who would replace their dead leader to come chasing after an escaped prisoner. He limped along, head down, thinking of how they would find a safe place to sleep for the night. Next to him Sarah gasped and stopped, tightening her grip on his arm.

When Dez looked up the sight that greeted him was so unexpected he thought he was hallucinating. Vroc, wet, muddy, and with dried blood on his flank, stood in their path as if he had been waiting for them for hours. Dez held out his hand to Sarah, assuring her that all was well as he approached the saark. Vroc looked the warrior over stoically. Finally, he put his forehead against the man's chest and gave a light push. Dez set his feet and pushed back. Satisfied that his rider was still strong, Vroc took two steps toward Sarah and snorted, eyeing her. She was scared, but somehow she knew she was being measured. She stepped forward and slowly reached out toward the beast. Vroc snorted a warning again, but she gently put her hand on the saark's snout. Vroc let her scratch him for a moment and then pulled away. Dez took his reins and mounted the saark. He pulled Sarah up behind him. Once settled Dez turned the beast toward the north and safety.

Wastelander: Not as They Appear

"Kill her," the simple words were shouted as if they were the vilest of curses and punctuated with a stone striking the young girl again. Her vision swam from the blows, making the ramshackle houses of the settlement blur in her vision.

The girl's light hair, matted with blood, covered her face. Her clothing was torn, and she was covered with the dust she was kneeling in. Blood, tears, and sweat were creating muddy rivulets in the fine power on her skin. The settlers were standing in a loose circle around her in the middle of the Wasteland village. All of them were ragged and dirty, testifying to a hard life trying to survive on the Waste. From this position, she felt the tremor in the ground before her assailants did.

"He's coming," she whispered.

Someone in the surrounding crowd heard her speak and rushed forward to kick her harshly, "No more of your curses!"

The girl tumbled, hard, into the dirt. When she tried to rise, the man kicked her hands out from under her. He lifted his arm to bring a stone down on her but paused as everyone heard what the girl felt moments before. Looking toward the sound, everyone could see two riders racing in their direction. One was a young woman, slight of build, mounted on a small horse. The other, a tall, well-built man, was riding what the villagers could only describe as a monster. The creature was a saark, a savage equine beast, all sharp hooves, and teeth. It had a coarse coat and deadly-looking curved horns that sprouted from the back of its head and curved forward to its nose. The beast's rider looked equally dangerous: tall, scarred, and carrying an array of weapons on his mount that many of the settlers had never seen before. He grasped the reins in one hand. The other arm ended in a metal-capped stump.

Dez and his sister Sarah had looked down at the village from the top of a low rise before riding down. The place was a typical Wasteland settlement, shanties, and huts constructed of cast-off materials scavenged from around the area. The buildings stood in a loose circle around a central meeting area with all doors and windows facing inward to make the settlement safer and easier to defend from raiders. Dez saw the crowd gathered in the center of the village, and they had obviously been stirred up about something. He could see them throwing stones at something, or someone, in the middle of the group. The mob parted for a moment, and he saw all he needed to see. Without a word to Sarah, he spurred Vroc, leaning forward as the saark took off from the hill. His sister followed as fast as her mare would carry her.

Dez and Vroc were moving fast between the buildings when the man kicked the girl. Dez saw him raise a rock over his head, ready to bring it down on the slight form lying in the dust at his feet. The onlookers parted as Dez rode through. He leaped from his saark to land between the girl and her assailant. Dez was unarmed, but he needed no weapons to intimidate the stone-wielding villager.

"Strong enough to kick a little girl, but not me?" Dez asked quietly, poking the man in the chest with his metal-capped stump. The villager dropped the stone and stumbled back. He looked around for support, but, between the huge warrior and his saark, the others were quickly losing their nerve.

"But, she's an abomination," the man stammered.

Dez kept his eyes on him.

"Can you stand, girl?" he asked loudly enough for her to hear. Sarah was already helping her to her feet. Dez heard his sister gasp behind him, and he turned, ready to defend her from whatever threat had arisen at his back.

He expected to see the villagers closing in on his sister, or something equally threatening. Instead, the girl stood with her back to him, facing Sarah. His sister had a hand over her mouth and a look of terror on her face. What could she be seeing, he thought, was the girl horribly scarred or deformed? He reached out and turned the girl around to face him. She was a pretty young girl, not yet a woman, with a soft, innocent face and blonde hair beneath the grime. He took a step back without realizing it, pulling his hand away like it had been burned. It was not her face, or her youth, that had everyone frightened. She had eyes of the brightest blue, intense and vibrant, and completely foreign in a world of only brown eyes and green, black and hazel. Hers were eyes that captured the essence of a sapphire and trapped it in the shining orbs of a child. The eyes of a witch. He shook off the fear of superstition and reminded himself that she was just a child.

"You're coming with me," Dez said softly, taking her firmly by the arm.

"Dez, she's a…" Sarah began.

"Nonsense," Dez cut her off, "Get your horse. We're leaving."

As Dez led the girl away, the villager he confronted before seemed to find a modicum courage.

"Good riddance," he spat at them, then picked up the stone to throw at their backs.

Dez turned. He pulled the girl behind him, and glared at the man. The man paled under the gaze of the massive warrior and his saark. He dropped the stone again and took an involuntary step back. The ringleader's loss of nerve seemed to be all the other villagers needed to finally break. They quickly found somewhere else to be. The leader stumbled away, wishing he could make himself invisible.

Dez led the girl to Vroc, and his sister mounted her own mare. He lifted the girl into the saddle and climbed up behind her, mildly surprised that she showed no fear around the savage saark. His sister crowded close as they rode away.

"Dez, I hope you know what you're doing," she whispered loudly.

"Just ride," he said. Strong as he was, he knew if the villagers found the courage to band together against him, he and his sister would be in trouble.

They rode a short distance up into the deserted hills above the town before Dez determined they would be safe. No one spoke until their camp was set up and the girl was settled in by a small fire. Finding wood on the Waste was always difficult so they had to carry their own, and a fire bigger than glowing coals tended to draw dangerous attention. Because of this Dez carried a bag of charcoal much like a blacksmith would use. Once they finished setting up camp Sarah pulled Dez away.

"What are we doing here brother? She's a witch."

"She's a little girl," Dez said flatly. On this subject, he was always immovable, ever since the killing of his parents and the kidnapping of his sister, Sarah, when they were children.

"You saw her eyes. We both know what that means," Sarah insisted.

"Look, Sarah, I've seen a lot of things in my life, but I've never seen a witch. What I did see was an entire village about to murder a little girl. I don't give a damn about old wives tales," Dez said firmly.

Sarah looked at Dez for a long moment, neither saying a word. He was the strongest, bravest man she had ever known. Since he had saved her from the warlord, Pontius, he had kept her safe. He was always confident and she had a hard time questioning his instincts. Finally, she nodded.

"I'll take her to get cleaned up. We passed a stream a little ways back."

He nodded and returned to camp to check on their mounts.

*   *   *

Sarah led the girl to the stream they had passed on the way to the camp. It was far enough away to give them some privacy, but close enough that Dez would hear her call if there was trouble. It was a sad little waterway fed by a spring somewhere in the hills. Sarah could see that it flowed to the village below, but likely dried up before reaching much farther.

"What's your name?" the girl asked as Sarah helped her out of her clothes.

"Sarah," she replied. When she helped the young girl into the water she felt guilty for her earlier comments. The girl was obviously young, younger than she originally appeared, and her body was covered in cuts and bruises. Sarah used sand from the streambed to carefully scrub the blood and filth from the girl's skin. The girl winced when Sarah's hand pressed too hard against a particularly nasty bruise.

"Sorry," Sarah said, her tone softer than before.

"You don't like me," the girl said quietly as Sarah tried to clean out the worst of the cuts. "It's all right. Everyone is afraid of me."

Sarah's hands faltered in their ministrations. She sounded like a little girl who was lost and had simply resigned herself to her lot in life. Guilt boiled up in the pit of Sarah's stomach and tears threatened at the corners of her eyes.

"What's your name?" Sarah asked softly, returning to her task of cleaning the girl up.

"Sarina," she answered. There was a note of surprise in the girl's voice.

"Well, Sarina, I'm not going to lie to you. You do scare me a little," Sarah smiled up at Sarina, receiving a slight smile in return. "I know for a fact though, you don't scare everyone."

Sarina looked in the direction of their camp. Neither of them could see Dez from the stream, but both of them could imagine the large man tending the mounts and arranging the camp.

"He's not afraid of anyone," Sarina said simply.

"No, not really," Sarah pulled Sarina's hand to get her to crouch in the water so she could rinse the girl off and wash her hair.

*   *   *

Dez tended to the little mare while Vrok looked on. The warrior considered his decision to bring the girl with them. He'd heard all the stories about the blue-eyed witches, but he rarely gave credence to stories like that. Dez believed what he saw with his own eyes. He had real monsters to worry about, and no time for those born of superstition. The villagers were the monsters this time. The thought that they might have killed the girl made his blood boil anew. The decision was easy with that in mind.

Dez finished with the mounts and moved to finish setting up their camp. They had very little in the way of possessions, but on the Waste that was to their benefit. The less they carried, the less likely they would be targeted by raiders. He was working on a simple meal when his sister and the girl returned.

"Dez, her name's Sarina," his sister announced as if presenting her for inspection. With all the dirt and blood washed off, she looked younger than he first thought.

"How old are you, girl?" Dez asked in his rough voice. He took note that she held his gaze without fear.

"I don't know," she replied.

"How do you not know?" Sarah asked.

"My parents left me behind a few years ago and left me behind. They never told me. I think they were scared of me, but couldn't do what most people do with blue-eyed children," Sarina said it as if talking about the weather. It was widely rumored that blue-eyed children were killed by their parents if their eyes remained that color after the first months of their lives. "I remember them arguing about it, but I was too young to understand."

Dez could see right away that, despite her young age, her hard life had made her grow up fast.

"You don't have anyone to take you in?" Sarah asked.

"No one," Sarina replied.

"We could take her to the Tower," Sarah said to Dez.

Dez saw the look on Sarina's face when the tower was mentioned.

"What's the matter, girl?"

"You saved me from that mob and now you want to get rid of me? Can't I come with you?" She looked at both of them, for the first time her calm demeanor breaking as she pleaded with them. "I can cook, mend clothes…"

Dez waved his hand and the words died on her lips. "The Waste is dangerous for a little girl, Sarina. You'd be safer with the sisters."

The girl's head drooped, and she nodded, letting her hair fall in front of her eyes. Sarah stepped up and put a hand on her shoulder.

"Don't worry about it," Sarina said softly, "I'm used to it." The girl walked to the small fire and sat down heavily, staring into the flames.

Dez could see the sympathy in his sister's eyes. The same sympathy he felt himself. This girl had been abandoned, neglected, and abused her entire life. Now her rescuers were talking about abandoning her again. He understood why she was upset, but he had to consider her safety over her feelings. She was only a child after all.

"Give the child time. She'll see the wisdom in it," Dez told his sister before they joined Sarina at the fire.

After a simple meal, Dez took first watch. The other two wrapped themselves in blankets and went to sleep. He moved a short distance away so his eyes could adjust to the darkness. He settled onto the stony ground with his axe laid across his knees. The night was quiet other than the faraway sounds of Wasteland predators and prey engaging in nature's mortal dance. His watch was uneventful, and he woke Sarah up for her turn with nothing to report.

* * *

Sometime during Sarah's watch, Dez was awakened. She was shaking him and saying his name softly.

"Dez, wake up. Something's wrong at the settlement," Sarah said.

Dez rolled to his knees at the quiet alarm in her voice. He quickly scanned their camp while he reached for his axe. There was no immediate danger. The mounts were calm and his sister was looking into the darkness. Sarina was sitting up as well, her head cocked to the side as if listening. He could hear it too at that point.

They were only a short from the settlement where they found Sarina, and sound carried well at night. Shouting, screams, and the sound of battle were faint hints of what was happening in the distance. At this hour that could only mean one thing. The settlement was under attack.

"Ravagers," Dez said, referring to the Wasteland raiders that preyed on settlers and travelers.

Dez got to his feet and ran to Vroc, Sarah and Sarina close behind. He looked down at them as he mounted.

"I'm going to see if there's any chance to help them," he said.

"I should go too," Sarina started to move toward Vroc to mount. The Saark snorted and stepped away.

"It's too dangerous, child," Dez insisted.

"I can help. Trust me."

Vroc seemed to be struggling with the decision whether to bite her or bolt, but the girl stood firm. Dez could tell something was different about her and Vroc could sense it too. Something in her blue eyes, eyes much too old for someone so young, told him to trust her.

"That was my home," she said softly, raising her hand to him.

"Dammit," Dez relented, against his better judgment, and forced Vroc to calm down and move toward Sarina. He took her hand and pulled her up behind him. "Sarah, you may as well come too. It's safer than staying here alone."

Sarah mounted her own horse, and they kicked their mounts into a gallop back in the direction of the settlement. They rode hard over the rocky ground, the sounds of battle becoming clearer over the pounding of hooves and the mounts' heavy breathing. Soon they were able to see an orange glow ahead and smell acrid smoke from a large fire.

The settlement came into view as they crested a small rise. The flames were eating at several buildings and casting a glaring backdrop to the carnage raging through the village. Dez and his sister reigned in at the crest of the rise and watched the scavengers at their grisly work.

The raiders were mostly men, dirty and dressed in patchwork clothing and cast-off pieces of armor. They were chasing settlers from their homes and cutting them down the men and elderly. The women and children they separated and herded into a frightened, shivering group. The children would be raised to swell the ranks of the ravagers, tortured and abused, their minds twisted until they turned out like their kidnappers. The women's fate would be short and brutal unless they proved cooperative, and able to bear children.

"Dez?" Sarah asked. The tone of her voice let him know what she wanted.

"There's too many. We need to get away before we are spotted," Dez had faced many challenges in his life, and killed many people that needed killing. Even he knew better than to face a raiding party of that size alone. Vroc side-stepped as Sarina leaped off his back, landing lightly on her feet.

"Sarina," Dez reached for the girl, but it was too late. Her swift feet had her out of reach.

"Damn!"

Dez kicked Vroc into a run, catching up to the girl, but when he reached for her she dropped to the ground. He rode past, and by the time he got the saark turned around she was on her feet and running toward the village. He could have sworn he heard her talking to herself when he reached for her.

Sarah was swinging around so they could pin her between their mounts and cut her off. If they got much closer to the village the raiders would surely see them, even with the fires ruining their night vision. The two riders bore down on the girl, circling to her front to block her run. That was about the time when Dez's world was turned upside-down.

As Sarah and Dez were closing in front of Sarina the girl stopped, threw her arms out, and shouted a word Dez had never heard before. He saw her blue eyes flash a bright sapphire right before the nightmares burst out of her body. The force of their passage lifted her bodily from the ground. She hung like that, back arched and limbs hanging limp, as things only seen in the most terrifying of dreams burst out of her. Her head was thrown back and staring at Dez through frightened blue eyes and her mouth gaped in a silent scream. The mounts screamed in terror - even

Vroc, who had never shied from anything - pitching their riders to the ground as they reared and bolted. Creatures made of darkness, engulfed in green smoke, swarmed over them, heading for the settlement. Their passing chilled Dez to the bone but otherwise left him untouched. Dez jumped to his feet after they passed and turned to look at the village. The creatures moved swiftly, entering the outer buildings at several different points.

For a moment everything was silent except for his breathing and the roar of the flames. Then all at once, the screams returned, but they were different. Where there had once been cries of pain, shouts, and the clash of weapons there was now only soul-piercing wails of fear and despair. Dez watched in horror as one of the dark spirits chased a raider toward the edge of the village. The raider stumbled, and the smoky being was upon him, then through him. The apparition passed right through his body, and as it exited it seemed to pull more black smoke with it. Dez could see the resemblance between the new smoke and the raider. The form let out a wail that turned Dez's blood to ice. It was a sound he had never heard before, nor wanted to again. The man's body was pulled along for a moment, attached to the smoky figure as if by a string which was suddenly cut. The body collapsed to the ground, dead, and the smoke dissipated as the wail faded away. Then the spirit creature returned to the town, looking for its next target.

Sarah let out a shuddering breath, and Dez turned to see her kneeling in the dirt, staring at the body. The terrible wailing continued through the settlement as he moved to his sister and put his arms around her. He forgot the last time he had been scared of anything, but what he was seeing was beyond anything he'd witnessed before. He could only imagine what she was feeling as she shook in his arms.

He looked over Sarah's shoulder at Sarina. The girl was standing again, still as a statue except for her eyes. The blue orbs were darting around as if she were trying to watch a hundred different things at once. He helped his sister to her feet and approached the girl. He waved his hand in front of her face, trying to catch her attention. Something about all of this made him loathe to touch her. Whatever she was looking at was beyond them. As Dez watched her, trying to decide what to do, she collapsed. He reacted with a warrior's quickness and caught her before she hit the ground. She was shaking and seemed to be unaware of anything around her. With her collapse, the wailing had stopped. The only sound was the roaring of flames from the burning settlement.

Dez looked back at the village. People were stumbling about in shock and confusion, but otherwise unharmed by the specters. All of the raiders he could see were dead, scattered among the bodies of their victims. Sarina's magic ended the raider's assault on the village, but it looked like the loss to the settlement would be staggering. Fires still raged, and there were too few settlers left to keep the place safe anymore. The survivors staggered about, some checking for friends and family members, others attempting to put out the fires. Dez looked down as Sarina stirred.

"Good to see you're still alive, girl," he said gruffly. She offered a weak smile and struggled to sit up.

"Dez," Sarah said in a warning tone. He looked up to see a few of the villagers approaching, led by the man Dez had first seen about to kill Sarina the day before.

"That was your work, witch?" The ringleader spat the word. Dez growled and started to get up, ready to finally put an end to the villager's attitude for good, but Sarina stopped him with a hand on his arm.

"Yes, that was me," she said hoarsely.

"Why?" He asked, a look of disbelief clear on his face.

"This was my home. I couldn't just sit by and watch," she replied, her voice regaining its strength as her body did.

The man nodded once, looking at the ground for a time, seeming to struggle with some decision. Finally, he sighed and scratched at his scalp. "It can still be your home. We could use your help around here."

Sarina studied him for a time as he kept his eyes on the dirt. After a minute of uncomfortable silence, he looked up.

"No," she said simply, turning on her heel and heading for Vroc, who had slowly approached them after the specters had vanished. The villager looked surprised. When Dez rose to his feet the look changed to fear, and he stepped back. Dez smiled at his discomfort and the situation itself.

"You don't deserve her. None of you do," he said, also turning to walk away from the village. His sister followed. They had helped the villagers as far as they were willing so they mounted up, Sarina behind Dez, and rode away from the ruined settlement.

* * *

Sarina looked up at the Tower of the Healers. It was a tall angular building, some castoff remnant of the ancient world still standing in the middle of the blasted Wasteland.

"They'll take care of you here," Dez placed his large hand on her shoulder. She could hear the apologetic tone in his voice.

"I know," she said softly, "Thank you Dez, Sarah, for everything."

"We'll come back to visit. Dez always needs to see the healers eventually," Sarah said with a smile. At that, Dez raised his eyes to look at one of the three healers that came out to meet them under the watchful gaze of their paladin guardians. Dez still kept his secret, even from Sarah. He looked away from the slight pain and longing in the eyes of the healer, Kara.

"I know," Sarina turned and smiled, giving Sarah a hug, then taking Dez's hand in farewell. No other words of goodbye were spoken. Sarina turned and walked to the three women in white that were waiting to take her into her new home.

Kara, the youngest of the three, took the girl's hand and nodded to Dez, giving him a brief smile. In that look, Dez felt the love she bore him, and he knew that no matter what Kara would look after Sarina as if the girl were her own child. He joined Sarah at the mounts, and they left the Tower to ride back into the dark Wasteland.

The Healer's Burden: A Wasteland Tale

The chaos of people shouting and cries of an angry beast penetrated Kara's slumber. She shifted on her rope cot and looked across the small stone cell at the narrow window. The scream rang out again, carried through the portal by the predawn air. It was unclear if the animal was hurt, but it was sure to wake everyone in the Tower.

Kara settled her bare feet on the cold stone floor and shivered as the chill air from the open window embraced her exposed body. She took two steps to cross to the cabinet and retrieved the simple robe and pulled it over her head. The rough wool settled around her legs and she slid her feet into the simple slippers that rested next to the wooden door of her cell.

All around Kara the Tower was beginning to come alive as she descended the worn stone steps to the main floor. The old stone walls were made of straight-cut blocks mortared together in even, straight lines. No one in Kara's time could replicate the construction and she often traced her fingers along the smooth lines as she walked the halls, wondering about the lives of the builders. Sisters were exiting their cells, bleary-eyed and full of questions, and armored paladins were rushing to the main floor as if the place were under attack. She hugged the wall as three knights, charged with the protection of the healers, rushed down the stairs. Their armor rattled and their swords clanked against metal plates as they went. Chaos buzzed around her but she was calm. Kara was always calm.

The scene in the courtyard was exciting and terrifying all at once. Six paladins, armed with swords, surrounded a saark. A creature out of a nightmare, a saark resembled a horse in head and body, but it was as large as the largest horse anyone had ever seen. That is where the similarities ended. Long curved horns, like those of a ram, curved down from the back of the animal's skull to end in lethal points. Razor sharp teeth and hooves were its weapon of choice, and their unpredictably wild temperament meant only the insane, or recklessly brave attempted to ride them. The equine beast was lashing out with hooves and sharp teeth, seeming intent on protecting the cloaked rider that was slumped against his neck. The rider must have been tied to the saddle, Kara realized, to remain mounted while obviously unconscious. Two of the paladins, Jessen and Kain, were trying to get a hold of the animal's bridle to take control of it.

"All this over one beast?" The Head Mother called from the top of the Tower steps that led to the large front door. Dressed much like Kara, except for a white sash that crossed her body from shoulder to waist, the elder seemed to command power with a simple look. Even the saark turned its attention to her while keeping the paladins at bay.

"Kill the beast so we can see to its rider," the older woman said.

The knights closed in on the saark and the beast reared violently. The cloak that had been covering the rider's head fell back with the movement. Kara recognized the rider instantly.

"Sarah?"

Kara rushed toward the struggling paladins, her head abuzz with questions and worry. Why was Sarah riding Vroc? Where was Dez? Was Sarah alive?

"Wait!" Kara shouted before the paladins could strike the beast.

The warriors hesitated as she approached the group with her arms held out to the sides. The officer in charge looked to the elder woman still standing on the stairs. At her nod, the squad backed off and made an opening for Kara. She passed between them without taking her eyes off the saark.

"Vroc!" Kara said firmly.

Turning one wild eye on Kara the beast stomped a sharp hoof and clawed at the dry ground of the courtyard.

"Vroc, we need to see to Sarah, but you have to calm down first," Kara explained. She stood close and reached out to try and calm him.

Vroc snorted again and nipped at her hand, his sharp teeth snapping together within a hair's breadth of her fingertips. She knew to expect that and was quicker. She brought her fist down on the soft spot between the animal's nostrils. He dropped his head like Dez said he would. She caught hold of the curved horns along the side of the saark's head and spoke softly to the beast.

"Vroc, you know me. You need to calm down now," she said, making soft shushing sounds as if calming an upset child. She nodded her head toward Sarah and two paladins moved to cut her out of the saddle.

*   *   *

Kara's morning routine rarely changed. She would roll out of her cot and stretch the kinks out of her neck and back. Her wash basin, with its rough cloth and cool water, stood across her small cell. She would rush to wash and get her goose-pimpled flesh into her robe in the cold months. During the hot months, she would take her time, hoping to catch a breeze from the window across her bare flesh while her skin was wet enough to make a difference. After slipping her feet into her plain slippers it was down to the chapel for prayers, then breakfast, and finally, rounds in the infirmary. Between rounds she studied in the library of recovered books and worked to educate Sarina, the young blue-eyed outcast Dez had brought to the Tower the year before. Every day the same, no adventure, little excitement, exactly the way the sisters liked it.

The morning after Sarah arrived, Kara rolled off her cot but found her legs caught in the light cover she used. Her sleep-addled mind flashed through a moment of panic before she realized it was not some nightmare grasping at her legs, but a sheet tangled in restless sleep. Finally, on her feet, she stretched - but the motion did little to work the kinks out of her sore body. The night had been long, and sleep far too scarce. She stepped to the lone cabinet and pulled out one of her two woolen robes and pulled it over her head, taking a moment to hug herself and enjoy the immediate increase in warmth. She slid into her slippers and left her cell for the chapel on the main floor.

Kara descended the stairs, her mind already fluttering from worry to frustration. She was worried about Dez and his sister, and everything about the day was testing her level of patience. A feeling sat in stomach like a lead weight, a dread that her life was starting to march down a new, chaotic path, no matter how hard she tried to rein it in. The floor of the tower she lived on was quiet, as was usual early in the day. She was an early riser and liked the feeling of solitude in the empty halls before life stirred in the Tower. It was still a couple of hours before the end of the night watch so most Sisters were still abed. It gave her time to dwell on all her worries. Was that good or bad, she wondered.

Kara knew worrying about things was useless so she forced herself to push the distressing thoughts to the back of her mind. Sarah was still unconscious from exhaustion and there was nothing she could do until her friend came out of it. The sisters knew to find Kara as soon as the patient woke up, so all she could do was try to go about her day as normally as possible.

Kara reached the chapel and settled into her usual place, facing the image of a woman wrought in polished brass. The ancient statue's features were no longer recognizable from ages of polishing by loving hands and the ravages of time, but the female form was unmistakable in the curve of the hips and soft rounding of breasts. Kara always felt at peace under the image of her Goddess and gazed at the smooth face, trying to imagine what its features may have looked like. She relaxed on the sandstone bench for a moment, finding calm in one of her favorite places. It was the reason she always rose early. The quiet in the sanctuary, sitting alone with her thoughts and prayers to the Goddess was what allowed her to forget the rigors of the day before and strengthen herself to face the one ahead.

Kara's peaceful reverie was destined to be short. Sarina ran into the chapel, knowing exactly where to find her mentor at any given time of the day. The young girl stopped next to the bench Kara was sitting on and fought to catch her breath. Kara waited patiently for the girl to gather herself.

"What is it, Sarina?" Kara asked when the girl had calmed herself.

"Sarah," the girl could barely contain the excitement as she shouted. "She's awake."

Sarina took the healer's hand and pulled her upright. She led Kara from the chapel at a run that nearly bowled over one of the other sisters making her way up the stairs. It was obvious the girl was relieved and excited, and Kara had a hard time maintaining her own composure. The pair rushed down the stone steps, passing several surprised sisters on the way. It was unusual to see anyone run in the Tower, especially Kara. They passed several sisters, and a pair of disapproving elder women, before reaching the infirmary.

*   *   *

The infirmary was a large room in the center of the Tower, second in size only to the dining hall. The open space was broken up by evenly spaced beds and privacy screens made of canvas. When Sarah was brought in, most of the beds were empty, so the young woman had most of the end of the hall to herself. Upon entering the room Kara could see her friend stirring while two sisters were attempting to tend to her. Kara and Sarina crossed the room to help.

"How long have I been sleeping?" Sarah's voice was on the verge of panic.

"A few hours, since Vroc brought you in last night," Kara explained. She tried her best to get Kara to lie back so the sisters could check her over.

"Too long," Sarah struggled to sit up.

"You are exhausted, and need to rest," Kara practically laid her entire body across the other woman's chest to get her to lie down. She looked at one of the other healers. "We may need to restrain her."

The other healers reached under the cot to retrieve the straps used to restrain difficult patients.

"No," Sarah said weakly. "Kara, it's Dez. He's dying."

"Wait," Kara said. One of the sisters was already attaching one strap to the woman's wrist but paused at Kara's command.

"What about Dez?" Kara was now starting to feel some of the panic that Sarah was obviously going through. She wanted to shake Sarah but satisfied herself with squeezing the woman's calloused hand. "What do you mean he's dying?"

"Manticore," Sarah said, going on to explain. "We stumbled into its den chasing a lizard that was meant to be dinner."

"Manticore…," Kara repeated the vile creature's name.

Sarah nodded and continued," Dez pushed me aside when it struck. He took the hit meant for me."

The pain in her voice was obviously fueled by the guilt she still felt over leaving Dez.

"Did he kill it?" Kara was trying hard to keep calm.

"No," Sarah shook her head. "He wounded the beast and it ran deeper into the cavern. I dragged him out and took him to the Sand Sage."

The Sand Sage was a hermit known by almost everyone in that area of the Wasteland. No one knew where he was from, but many people went to him for healing, potions, and fortune telling. The healers in the white tower felt he was a crazy old man taking advantage of other people, and he had no love for the sisters himself.

"How long?" The healer was already doing mental calculations.

"One day to the Sage, then three here," Sarah said.

Kara was thinking about time, dosage, and body weight while Sarina comforted their friend. She had never treated such an affliction before but she knew from her studies that the poison was deadly without the proper antidote. She recalled entries in her books on the proper treatment, and location of the ingredient she would need.

"We will need to leave immediately," Kara's voice was calm despite the panic that was threatening to rise in her and take over. Healers were all trained to maintain control in a crisis, to give orders with confidence and project that calm to others. That training was her only shield against the turmoil boiling inside her.

"Leave?" The Head Mother said behind Kara. "And where is it you think you are going?"

Kara turned to the old woman who ruled the healer's Tower. She'd entered the infirmary silently while Kara was focused on her patient. The elder's mouth was pinched, as usual, like she had eaten something foul. Her dark eyes always looked like she was considering something awful and those eyes were fixed on Kara. The woman's gaze could melt stone, as some of the younger healers gossiped.

"Mother, you remember Sarah and Dez," Kara began. The older woman's expression darkened at the mention of the Wasteland wanderer. The younger healer stood firm, back straight. Kara continued, "They were attacked by a manticore four days ago," she said. Fear was threatening to break through her shield. "Dez was hurt and needs our help."

"Four days? The man's most likely to be dead before you get to him," the elder said calmly. She looked at Sarah.

"Why didn't you bring him here?"

"He was in too much pain to ride," Sarah said.

"I'm afraid you will have to let your brother go dear, it's been far too long," the Head Mother said sadly.

"Dez is too strong to be dead," Sarah said defiantly. She started to sit up again.

The healers tried to push her back but she thrust them forcefully away. The sisters were no match for the warrior's strength so they backed off. All except Kara. The young healer helped her friend stand.

"I'm willing to take the risk," Kara said.

"I can't allow that dear, you are needed here."

"With all respect Mother, I am going," Kara said.

Sarina watched the exchange, wide-eyed and proud of her mentor. At that last, she stepped up to stand by the healer.

"I'm going as well," the girl said.

"No, it's too...," Sarah started to say but Kara put a hand on her arm and she fell silent.

"Sarina, I'm going to need you here to prepare for when we get back," the healer said. "There's a book in my room that covers the treatment of poisons. Read the chapter on recovery and make sure you have everything ready."

The girl looked like she might argue but stopped, her shoulders slumped in defeat. She nodded her acceptance finally.

"I know you want to help Dez," Kara touched the girl's cheek to get her to look up. "I promise this is no busy work."

Sarina nodded again. She gave Sarah a hug and rushed off to begin her tasks.

Kara looked to the Head Mother and the two stared at each other for several heartbeats. The young healer could sense her elder's will, the strength of the venerable healer who was considered one of the most powerful people in the Waste. For years everyone in the Tower followed her orders without question. Kara was questioning now and it terrified her. She did her best to hide it, and imagined she saw a flash of respect in the upward twitch of the elder's lips before she spoke.

"I see you are set on this course, but you will take a pair of paladins with you," the Head Mother said firmly.

Kara was willing to take the compromise as a win but Sarah spoke up before the healer could thank her teacher.

"The last thing we need is a couple of your knights slowing us down," Sarah said defiantly.

The Head Mother looked at her student, then the warrior next to her. She took the measure of the exhausted woman being held up by her friend.

"Sarah, you are so exhausted you can barely stand and Kara has never left the Tower alone," there was a note of finality in that statement.

"We'll take all the help we can get, thank you Mother," Kara said before anyone else could argue.

The elder nodded and left the infirmary. Kara turned to the other two healers and waved them away while she helped Sarah get dressed.

"Sarah, you know we never leave the Tower without an escort," Kara said gently while she helped the warrior out of the wool shift she was put in when they brought her to the infirmary.

"You have an escort," Sarah tapped her chest while the healer handed her underclothes to put on.

"I know on your worst day you're a match for anyone, but there's a lot that could go wrong and I cannot fight with you," Kara explained while she helped her friend pull on a pair of leather riding pants.

"I know, you're forbidden, but they will slow us down."

"No slower than I'll be. They'll dress light, and we'll have fast horses," Kara said.

Sarah dropped it and let the healer help her finish dressing. She put up a brief fight when Kara insisted she eat, but her friend assured her they had time since provisions had to be gathered and their mounts prepared.

* * *

Kara was lashing her pack to her mount's saddle when Sarah exited the Tower and descended the stone steps to the yard. The warrior looked much better after her rest and hot food but was still moving slowly. Kara finished securing the pack and moved to help her friend into Vroc's saddle.

"Someone managed to tend to Vroc?" Sarah asked, looking the saark over with a critical eye.

"They called me after he bit a stable hand and a paladin. I did the best I could."

While Kara helped the warrior mount, two men led their own horses into the yard. They were both dressed in riding leathers and light armor.

Each had a bow strapped to his saddle and a sword on his hip. The healer noticed Sarah looking each over with a critical eye and a frown. The paladins took note of the scrutiny as well.

"Lady Sarah, I am Sir Toren and my squire, Wen," Toren indicated the younger man next to him. "The Lady Karamin has briefed us. We are at your disposal."

"Squire?"

"Near to having my spurs My Lady," Wen said, giving a slight nod of deference.

"Wonderful," Sarah growled, kicking her heels into Vroc's flanks to send the saark leaping into a gallop. The others were forced to scramble to mount and catch up.

*   *   *

The first day's ride was hard on Kara. She had never ridden more than a couple miles at a time, and her tender buttocks were afire with pain. Despite that she rode for hours without complaint or requests to stop for her sake. When they did stop for the night she moved slowly, limping from task to task and not sitting down. Sarah and the squire were tending the mounts while Kara and Sir Toren prepared a light meal over the low fire.

"What is our plan Lady Karamin?" Toren asked while he stirred the boiling pot.

"My patient will need fresh panacea root from the Karsh Foothills," Kara said, looking to the west.

"That's a day's ride from here My Lady."

Kara nodded slowly, still staring out into the night.

"Will we be in time?" Toren persisted.

Kara swallowed, biting back the fear and uncertainty.

"I hope so, Sir Toren." She managed to keep her voice calm.

"Hope so what?" Sarah asked, having returned from the mounts.

Squire Wen crouched to help finish up the meal while Toren removed the light metal plates of his armor.

"Sarah, the plant we need for Dez," She stopped when Toren looked up with a raised brow. "The plant your brother needs grows in the foothills another day west of here. I pray we are able to get it to him in time."

"Dez is strong. We'll make it in time." Sarah's face betrayed her doubt, though her voice was firm.

"We could ride out after we eat," Wen suggested.

Sarah shook her head and turned to lay out her bedroll. Toren chuckled at Wen's look of confusion.

"I'm sure Lady Sarah wants nothing more than to ride on," the paladin began. "Only that daemon mount of hers can see in the dark though, and only fools ride the Wasteland on a moonless night."

Squire Wen blushed and nodded.

"I should have considered that, Sir Toren."

Kara left the two men to talk and walked slowly to where Sarah was shaking out her blankets.

"You're moving a little slow," Sarah noted without looking up.

"I've never been in the saddle this long," Kara said, grimacing when a sore muscle in her leg cramped.

The healer shook out her bedroll near Sarah's.

"You're right, Dez is strong. We'll make it in time," Kara said, smoothing the blankets out on the ground.

Sarah watched the healer for a moment before speaking.

"You're just as worried as I am."

Kara met the warrior's eyes and nodded. At that moment the two shared the depth of their feelings for Dez, an understanding that both would do whatever it took to save him. They connected as a family might, without exchanging another word. The moment was broken by the nervous neighing from the horses and Vroc's growls coming from the picket line. Squire Wen started to get up to check the mounts but Sarah waved him down.

"Vroc probably smelled food and is making the others nervous," Sarah said. "I'll go check."

The tension in the camp rose as Sarah moved away from the fire's dim light. Sir Toren stood and cocked his head to listen, putting his back to the fire to let his eyes adjust to the dark.

"Tend the pot," the paladin said quietly to Wen while he scanned the night around the camp.

Kara was staring in the direction Sarah had disappeared to when she saw movement in the shadows to her left, behind Toren. The knight turned quickly when he saw Kara's eyes dart to the space behind him. Whatever she'd seen was gone. Toren turned to her with a silent question in his eyes. She shrugged and shook her head but something moving in the dark to Toren's right caused her to jump.

Toren turned again but the beast in the dark was faster. The brindle-furred monster leaped out of the shadows and caught Toren's shoulder in its claws, taking him to the ground. The healer caught a brief glimpse of the creature before the two went down in a rolling heap of fur and flesh.

Wen shouted in surprise and ran for his spear at the same time the healer called out for Sarah. The squire turned to help Toren when the two adversaries rolled apart and came to their feet. The paladin had already removed most of his metal armor and his chest and face were covered in bleeding scratches and dirt. The creature itself was like something out of Kara's nightmares. A large feline body, covered in coarse brindled fur, was topped with a head that bore an almost human face and a mouthful of jagged fangs. The monster's body ended in a scorpion-like tail that waved back and forth slowly over the its back, following Toren's movements. When the squire stepped close, nervously clutching his spear in both hands, the beast turned to be able to see both men.

"Protect Kara," Toren said hoarsely, keeping his eyes on his enemy.

Wen backed away slowly, putting himself in front of the healer. Kara had risen to her feet and watched the confrontation with rising anxiety. She could hear the horses crying out in fear, and the saark in anger, while Sarah's cursing carried over the noise in the dark. Kara took it all in. The moment seemed to last forever before everyone moved again.

Toren was the first to act, stepping to the left before he lunged right in an attempt to take the manticore off guard. The creature seemed to fall for the tactic, stepping to follow the paladin's feint, but when Toren shifted and committed to his strike the monster's tail came around and struck hard at the back of the man's neck.

The knight screamed and fell to the dirt. The manticore lunged forward to rip out the paladin's throat with its jagged teeth and silence the man's screams. Before Kara could move Wen jumped forward and thrust the spear deep into the manticore's shoulder. The monster snapped the spear shaft with a swipe of a massive paw and reared up before the now-unarmed squire.

Kara was so focused on the doomed squire that she missed seeing Sarah rushing through the dark. The warrior hit Wen around the waist in a running tackle that sent both sprawling in the dust. The manticore was as surprised as Kara, which gave Vroc the opportunity to attack. The freed saark charged out of the dark from the manticore's flank, lowered his head and slammed his curved horns into the beast's side. The brindled monster rolled across the camp and the saark reared above the fallen creature, trumpeting a challenge and raking the air with his sharp hooves.

The manticore stumbled to its feet with a stunned look on its too-human face. Vroc set his feet and lowered his head again to glare at the beast. Sarah had already pulled herself off of Wen and was stalking around their enemy's flank. As far as Kara could tell the monster was oblivious of the warrior coming up behind.

The saark pawed the ground, and kept the manticore's attention while Sarah stalked closer. Kara tried to watch all three, her eyes glued to the scene in morbid fascination, but even she was left breathless at the speed of her friend when Sarah finally attacked.

Vroc shifted his weight to the left, drawing the manticore's attention further from Sarah. As soon as the monster shifted to follow the saark, Sarah struck. She brought her heavy blade down in a two-handed stroke that severed the creature's tail clean through at the base. The night echoed with a human-like roar of pain as the manticore turned to lash out at the new threat. Kara, covering her ears, was thankful to see her friend dodge away. The raking claws found only empty air.

As Sarah back-peddled to avoid the next strike, Vroc reared and brought his sharp hooves crashing down on the mangled hind end of the creature. The manticore screamed again and collapsed onto its destroyed rump. Wen rose up, clutching the broken spear shaft. While the monster struggled with the rear half of its body that refused to respond the squire drove the broken point of the shaft into the creature's neck with all the force he could muster. The splintered wood pierced the manticore's hide with a sickening wet sound and a spray of hot blood. The creature shook and coughed once before collapsing at in the dirt, finally stilled.

While the monster lay in its pooling blood Kara rushed to Sir Toren's side. The paladin was unmoving, his eyes staring up at the night sky through a ruined and bloody face. Kara was unsure if it had been his gruesome wounds or the manticore's venom that killed him. She touched his eyes to close them. She was struck by the image of Dez lying dead at her feet rather than Toren. Her stomach tightened in fear at the brief vision before she could banish it from her mind.

"Dead?"

Kara looked up into Sarah's eyes and saw her friend had been thinking the same thing. Kara nodded and stood.

"We should move. Dez is running out of time," Sarah urged. The warrior looked back at the slain monster and frowned.

"What about the horses, and the dark?" Wen asked, clearly shaken and grieving, but trying to hold it together.

"We'll have to risk it," Sarah said.

Wen nodded and stumbled into the darkness toward the picket line to retrieve the horses. Kara stood and approached her friend, who was still staring at the brindle corpse with a strange look on her face.

"What is it, Sarah?" The healer asked.

"This isn't the same one," Sarah said quietly, like she was talking to herself rather than the healer.

"Same one? What do you mean?" She asked, her tone filled with dread after Sarah's words.

Sarah took her eyes off the beast slowly, as if she was coming out of a trance.

"It's not the manticore that struck Dez. My brother took half the beast's paw," Sarah clarified. "We were tracked by a different one. The wounded monster is still out there somewhere."

Kara realized why Sarah was so on edge. Manticores were relentless hunters, able to track prey within hundreds of miles of their dens. They were also mildly intelligent and tended to seek out anyone foolish enough to attack and leave the monster alive. They were usually solitary until they chose a mate. Once they did, they often hunted in pairs to take down larger prey for their young.

"We need to get out of here," Sarah said. She moved without waiting for a response. She reached her gear and started shoving things into her pack.

Squire Wen returned with the three horses and they packed up the camp without another word. They took a few moments to gather stones to protect the fallen paladin's body until they could return to see to it properly.

"Stay close, Vroc can see well enough to lead us. It will be light before we reach the hills," Sarah said.

Wen looked nervous but mounted and took up the reins of Toren's mount. Kara climbed into her saddle, gritting her teeth at the pain. She guided her mount in close to the squire's, hoping the closeness would comfort both of them. Nights on the Wasteland were usually quiet but that night was silent as a grave. The dead predator behind, and a live one out there somewhere made the darkness around feel sinister. The air was still, and stifling, and if not for the clip of their mount's hooves and the creak of the saddles they could hardly tell they were moving. None of them talked and they used a rope tied to Vroc's saddle to keep the horses generally following in a line.

As the sky lightened with the coming dawn the riders could see the foothills looming ahead. The sight of the Wasteland, with the blasted and barren landscape always saddened Kara, but in the predawn it was almost beautiful. Everything was cast in grays and blacks, giving the world around her a clean, new look. The sounds of life were beginning again around them, what little wildlife inhabited the dusty waste. The sounds of the living started to dispel some of the horrors of the previous night.

"We harvest the panacea from the top of that cut where the stream comes down," Kara said, pointing to a ravine that divided the hills ahead and to the right of their path.

"Let's get to it then," Sarah said, kicking Vroc into a canter.

Kara and Wen followed Sarah up the ravine toward the cut in the hills. Like all small waterways entering the Wasteland from the surrounding hills and mountains, the streambed they rode next to was mostly dry. Less than a mile into the blasted desert, further from the hills, it would be completely barren. When rain fell in the highlands the streams would fill so fast that people or animals caught in them could be swept away. The life-giving flow was always fleeting, as the parched ground soaked much of it up and the relentless sun baked off whatever was left.

The dry streambed was a blessing and a curse for the three riders. It meant the only fresh water they could rely on was what they were carrying, but it also meant no animals flocking to the water source or the dangerous predators that followed. With that thought in her mind, Kara scanned the dawn sky nervously, remembering there could still be a manticore hunting them. She let out a sigh of relief seeing the blue expanse empty as far as she could see in any direction.

"How far up does the plant grow?" Sarah asked over her shoulder.

"Up where the ground is healthy enough, close to the streambed," Kara pointed to an area ahead where they could see pathetic patches of wiry grasses and bushes clinging to life in the hard ground.

Sarah scanned the several hundred yards between them and the vegetation, then the sky around. Even in the mountains, healthy ground was an illusion. Hardly anything that grew in the heights was edible, so most people lived in the lowlands where careful cultivation could provide enough for a family to get by.

"No birds in the sky today," Kara commented.

"Or beasts on the ground," Sarah added.

Squire Wen jerked around as if all the hells were chasing him and scanned the sky nervously.

"Relax, if the beast was close enough to see he'd already have you," Sarah said without looking at him.

That did nothing to reassure the young man. The party continued up the draw, scanning the sky and surrounding hills despite Sarah's comment. When they reached the top of the ravine, where the moister soil allowed plants to grow, Kara stopped and dismounted.

"I'll need a few minutes to locate the root," the healer pulled a small shovel from behind her saddle.

Sarah nodded and gestured for Wen to cover the path behind them, while she turned and guided Vroc a few yards ahead to get a better view of the area.

Kara could feel the pressure and anxiety settle heavily on her shoulders when she was left alone to her search. She knew what to look for, but it could take some time to find the plant tops that gave away the buried treasure. She knew time was short, but forced herself to dismiss the idea that it may have already run out.

She thought about Dez as she searched, and what the man meant to her. She'd lived a sheltered life at the tower, so she had no experience with relationships like theirs. Still, she believed she loved him. She thought he loved her as well, though he never said it. He knew it was an impossible prospect and wanted to avoid putting pressure on her, so she believed. If he had other reasons, she was unaware of them. When he visited, there was always an intensity in his eyes that made her breath catch in her throat. There was a pain behind them as well, as if there was something he wanted to say but failed to find the words. He knew the rules as much as she did; the healers must remain untouched and unbonded. They belonged to the Goddess and their patients, not any one person. Should they give themselves to someone physically they would lose what healing powers the Goddess had bestowed upon them. No one remembered the last healer who had lost her powers that way. In moments of weakness, she wondered if it was only a superstition. Even so, to take the chance might mean she would lose the ability to help others. She avoided entertaining the idea for long.

Her thoughts were interrupted when she spotted what she was looking for. She saw the tiny green shoots reaching through the rocky soil to gather what light they could. Kara moved quickly, brushing away the loose rocks and dirt to better see the root top. She had to be careful to avoid breaking the skin of the tuber. If she slipped and cut the root with her digging tool the plant would lose its healing qualities as the precious fluids seeped out.

Once the healer uncovered enough of the root to guess at its size she slowly dug around the plant. The process took far longer than she liked, but if she damaged it, she would have to find another. After a tense few minutes of careful scraping and digging, Kara pulled the precious plant from the ground and brushed away the clinging soil to inspect the skin for damage. She said a quiet prayer of thanks to the Goddess when she found no cuts. Her heart leaped in her chest and she gathered her things and ran for her horse, calling Sarah's name.

Vroc's angry cry caught her attention and time seemed to slow down. Sarah was riding hard for her companions but the sight above nearly stopped the healer's heart. Another manticore, larger than the last and missing one forepaw, was bearing down on the saark and his rider from the air. The women's eyes met and Kara shared a moment in time with the warrior that said all that needed to be said. It was the only goodbye they had time for before Sarah shouted for the healer to run and wheeled Vroc around to confront the winged monster.

Part of her wanted to stay and help her friend, but Kara knew there was nothing she could do. Sarah was buying her time to get away and reach Dez with the healing root. Tears sprang to her eyes as she ran for the mounts and Squire Wen. The idea of losing Dez weighed heavy on her, but losing Sarah as well was too much to bear. When she neared her mount, she could see Wen rushing toward her from farther down the slope. He was looking past her and had his sword in hand, guiding his horse in a headlong run up the ravine.

"No!" Kara shouted in a broken voice. "Wen, I need you with me."

Wen slowed his horse, looking down at Kara uncertainly.

"My Lady?" Wen was confused by what he was seeing.

"We have to go Wen," Kara reached her mount and remembered she'd dropped her digging tools. She tucked the root carefully into one of her saddlebags, glad she had the presence of mind to keep hold of it, and pulled herself into the saddle.

"We can't leave her," Wen said. He was clearly anxious to help in the fight.

Kara looked up at the battle at the top of the cut. She understood Wen's desire to help. The winged beast was diving down at saark and rider again and Sarah held her sword low, ready to strike when the monster was close.

"We must. She is buying us time and I need you with me," Kara kicked her horse into a canter before the squire could protest further. Wen's training took over and he grabbed up the reins of the extra horse and followed the healer.

* * *

Kara was plagued by guilt and fear as she made the headlong dash out of the hills with Wen. She felt guilty leaving Sarah and worse for feeling relief that the warrior bought them time to escape. Her fear pushed her to rush toward the hermit's home with her precious cargo. She leaned against her horse's neck and kicked the mount faster, hoping the squire could keep up. If Sarah was going to sacrifice herself, the healer would do her best to make it mean something.

When they reached the flat wastes below the hills Kara kicked her frightened animal again, urging it into a ground-churning gallop. The sound of grunting and pounding hooves told her Wen was keeping up. She felt the small hairs on the back of her neck rise as if the manticore would drop down on her at any moment. She kept her eyes forward and her head low as the horse's hooves pounded away the miles.

They pushed their mounts hard until Wen finally got Kara's attention. She reigned in her lathered mount and looked around, worried for a moment they might be facing a new danger. She saw they had left the hills so far in the distance she could barely make out their shapes. The horses hung their heads when they stopped and Wen looked like he might fall out of the saddle at any moment. Seeing him reminded her own body to tell her she was tired and sore as well. Their long ride through the night and dash down the mountain had taken its toll.

She stood in the saddle and looked around the blasted landscape while Wen did what he could for the horses. She knew of the hermit Sarah mentioned before. He lived in a hovel under the branches of a gnarled, ancient tree. The tree had somehow survived the devastation of the old wars and stood as a landmark in the Waste. It grew so massive that, like the Tower of the Healers, it could be seen for miles on the Wasteland. Its roots ran so deep that it found nourishment that would never reach the surface to nurture any other life but the tree.

Finally, after what seemed an age, Kara spotted the tops of the tree on the horizon to the north. The heat waves from the dry ground had obscured it and she had to squint to make out the branches in the distance. She was an inexperienced traveler but guessed their destination to be more than a couple hours ride. She looked to the south and knew the Tower rose above the Waste in that direction, and farther away. They were close, and Dez was short on time.

"We have to go," Kara said absently.

"My Lady, the horses need rest," Wen said.

"No time. We're close."

She finally lowered her eyes to look at the squire and the horses. They were all on the verge of collapse, but she knew the guilt would be unbearable if Dez died while they rested. Sarah and Toren's sacrifice and Dez's life meant too much to her.

"Your horse is likely to fall before you get there," Wen said.

"Then I'll walk," Kara gathered her mount's reins in preparation to leave.

"I won't be able to keep my oath if you ride ahead My Lady. My mount will collapse if we continue," the squire said.

She looked to his winded horse, then her own. There was no denying his words.

"You stay and rest the two you have and catch up when you can. I release you from your oath until you are able to return," Kara said.

The order of paladins who protected the healers took their oaths seriously. To release Wen from his was such a foreign idea that if he were a full paladin he may have refused. She would have to remember to leave that out of any report if they both made it back to the Tower. She could see him struggle with the decision. His inexperience and growth left him unprepared for the weight of it. She was his superior and he had not yet taken his oah which included a vow to protect the healers, even from themselves. Finally, he relented.

"At least take Toren's mount, he hasn't been carrying anyone," Wen held out the reins of the spare horse.

Kara dismounted and took the new mount by the bridle. She rubbed the horse's nose before taking the reins and mounting.

"No heroics, Squire. If that monster follows," Kara paused. The idea of Sarah being dead took her voice away for a moment. That would be the only way the warrior would let the monster follow them. She took a deep breath and continued.

"If you see the beast you run," she waited for Wen to nod his agreement. "When these two are rested enough, ride to that tree."

She pointed to the landmark in the distance.

"Yes, My Lady."

There was apprehension in his voice and for a moment Kara pitied him. She put it aside, however. It was time for Wen to prove he was worthy of knighthood. If they made it back she would be sure he did. Kara nodded after regarding the squire for a moment. Then she mounted and turned the horse's head toward the distant tree and set off.

*   *   *

"Thank you, Goddess," Kara said softly when the hovel near the base of the giant tree came into view.

After a couple hours of uneventful riding, she saw the patchwork shack crouching under the massive, gnarled tree like some large, skulking rodent. There were a few openings in the walls to let in air, and the slanted roof looked like it would let in more rain than it kept out. Not that the Waste got much rain anyway. Seeing no movement, she assumed the hermit must be inside, tending to Dez. She kicked the horse to make the last few yards in a dash.

When they reached the tree she pulled up and jumped off before her mount stopped completely. She stumbled, kicking up a cloud of dust, and fell to her hands and knees. The hard, stony ground cut her palms but she ignored the pain and climbed to her feet. She brushed her hands against her white robes, leaving behind red trails on the dusty fabric. For a moment the pain and weariness threatened to overwhelm her. She'd hardly slept since Sarah arrived at the Tower days ago. She took a deep breath, leaning against her mount a moment before shaking herself.

Ignoring the stinging wounds on her hands she opened the saddlebags and retrieved the precious root stored inside. She rushed to the hovel, moving around to what she assumed was the front. When she rounded the corner of the ramshackle dwelling, she saw a terrible scene of destruction. It looked like the place had been torn apart by something huge. A sheet of metal and wood lay in the dirt several feet away from the building. Kara assumed it was what passed as a door to cover the only opening large enough for a person to enter. Something huge and powerful had torn the door off its hinges and cast it aside, then proceeded to tear at the opening and metal around it. The ground was churned up near the doorway and Kara stumbled on the rutted dirt as she rushed inside.

Under the cooler shadows of the roof, the place was a wreck. Broken furniture and the hermit's meager belongings were scattered around the opening, but only within a few feet of it. It was as if something too large to get through the door made a mess attempting to reach something, or someone inside. The healer scanned the interior of the hut, which consisted of one room. There was no sign of Dez or the old man who lived under the tree. She was at a loss, all her hope dashed like the broken pottery on the floor. Her protector, her friend, and the squire all likely dead for nothing.

"Led the beastie away I did," called a hoarse, shaky voice from outside.

Kara turned from the destruction to look at the approaching man through the open doorway. The hermit was stooped and crooked as the limbs of the tree he lived under. He wore dirty patchwork robes and used a stick, as twisted as his own back, to support himself. He smiled a gap-toothed smile, meant to look just this side of senile, but Kara knew better.

"Where is Dez?"

Kara did her best to hide her distaste for the witch-doctor. Most in the Wastes simply called him The Old Man. He was a con artist as far as the healers were concerned, and none in the Tower approved of his experimental approach to healing.

"Hah! I buried your friend and led the beastie away," the hermit shouted. He cackled with glee and hopped about in a circle. His dance belied his decrepit appearance.

Kara felt like she was punched in the gut. She nearly dropped her precious cargo when her knees failed. The old man crossed the space between them faster than she thought possible and took her arm before she fell.

"Here, let me show you," the hermit smiled his gap-toothed smile and pulled her toward the back of the hovel.

She looked at the hermit when he took her arm. For an instant there was a flash of sanity, and possibly sympathy in his eyes. By the time she saw it though, it was gone. The old man led her back into the chaos of his home. His bony fingers bit into her flesh painfully. Part of her was repulsed by his touch, but another part was thankful because it helped her focus. Her mind took stock of her situation, which seemed to have turned into recovery rather than healing. She was already working through the logistics of recovering Sarah and Sir Toren as well and returning everyone to the Tower for proper burial.

The hermit left her standing in the middle of the small dwelling and moved to the back wall. He pulled bedding and junk away from a spot on the floor.

"Put him safe in the ground I did," the old man muttered to himself while he worked.

The word safe brought her out of her reverie to regard the old man. Why would he say safe, she thought? Was the hermit playing some game with her? She watched him uncover a sheet of rusted metal and moved to help lift it. Before the metal was fully pulled away the stench hit her and caused her to almost lose her grip on the metal plate. She bit the inside of her cheek to keep from gagging and continued to lift, dreading what was about to be revealed.

"Big boy's grown ripe, he has," the old man cackled.

Kara's patience with the hermit was spent but she pushed away the angry retort that came to mind and instead gave the metal an angry shove. It flipped off of whatever it covered and onto a pile of broken furniture that had once been a table and chair. Beneath the steel sheet was a hole that served as a pantry. Dez's body was crumpled in the too-small space among a sparse stock of roots and edible plants. The warrior looked smaller than the last time she had seen him. His expression was one of severe pain and his body was still covered in a sheen of sweat. She'd hoped he would have found peace in death after the trials of his life. It seemed her hope had been dashed. Her breath caught in her throat as she gathered herself for the task at hand.

"Can you help me get him out?" Kara asked after a moment.

The old man nodded, bending down to reach into the hole. The healer leaned in and when she touched Dez's shoulder she was surprised to find his skin still hot with fever. She got her hand under the warrior's shoulders while the hermit took hold of his legs. Kara lifted with all her strength, knowing she would need it to get the heavy man out of the hole.

Dez took a shuddering breath and moaned in pain when they lifted him. The old man laughed his grating glee and Kara nearly dropped Dez in surprise. His breathing was so shallow she'd missed it before. She cried in relief but managed to get Dez down on the floor gently.

"Boil water, now," Kara commanded, stepping into the role of commanding healer.

The old man grumbled but did what he was told. He got a fire going and put on a kettle of water. Kara righted the small table after pulling it out from beneath the metal plate. She managed to locate a clean cup among the damaged crockery and retrieved the root from where she set it down. She set the root on the table and carefully peeled away the outer skin with her knife.

By the time she had a generous amount of the root ball shaved and in the bottom of the cup the hermit approached with the steaming kettle. She took it and poured the boiling water into the cup and slowly stirred it with her knife. When she was satisfied, she held it up and said a soft prayer to the Goddess. The hermit rolled his eyes but kept his tongue.

Kara sat on the floor near the warrior's head and set the cup nearby. She gently pulled Dez's shoulders into her lap and rested his head in the crook of her arm. She could feel the heat rolling off his feverish skin. Picking up the cup, she held it to his lips while the old man looked on.

"Come back to me Dez," Kara said softly as she poured a trickle of the steaming liquid into his mouth.

She massaged his throat to make him swallow, but all of what she gave him spilled out of the side of his lips. She cradled his head like an infant and tried again, whispering prayers and encouragement. Finally, her ministrations coaxed the man to swallow a small amount of the medicine. He coughed and lost some of the fluid but Kara calmed him as she would a child and poured more into his mouth. When she managed to get Dez to finish the cup she set it down and looked up. The witch doctor was watching with a look of both sympathy and respect in his eyes. The look vanished almost as soon as she saw it.

"So, you've done your mumbo-jumbo. It's time to clear out of my house," the old man said.

He moved around the place, picking up broken dishes and righting furniture. He pointedly ignored her while he attempted to restore order to his home. Kara rocked Dez and prayed quietly over him, in no rush to move. A noise outside brought both of them to a frozen silence.

Kara slowly lowered her charge to the floor. She picked up her knife, untrained as she was, and slowly rose to her feet. She knew the repercussions should she take a life but, with Dez lying helpless, loss of the Goddess's blessings may be her only option. She prayed that whoever or whatever was outside could be scared off without a fight. The image of the injured manticore sprang to mind and her knees grew shaky but she turned toward the doorway. Her head was tilted, ear toward the door as she stepped between the comatose warrior and whatever danger was outside. She saw the hermit pick up a large piece of firewood from near the hearth.

"Kara?" A familiar voice called uncertainly from outside.

The knife fell from the healer's nerveless fingers and she rushed outside. A battered and bloody, but very much alive, Sarah was leading an equally disheveled Vroc. Behind her, Wen was holding the reins of a pair of exhausted horses. The healer threw herself into Sarah's arms, holding her friend close in relief.

"Dez?" Sarah asked quietly.

"Still alive," Kara stepped back and pulled the woman into the hut with her.

"Oh, go ahead. Let anyone in," the old man grumbled.

"I got the panacea into him but he is still unconscious."

Sarah kneeled next to her brother. She could see that his breathing was steadier than before and they both let out a sigh of relief.

"We need to move him soon," Kara said.

"Is that safe?"

The warrior wiped her brother's forehead with her sleeve. There was new blood on her clothes and it left a smudge on his pallid skin.

"It will have to be. I've done all I can here," the healer said. "And you need to be seen to as well."

Sarah looked herself over and seemed surprised at her appearance. Between the mud, blood and torn clothing, she was barely recognizable.

"Wen, go get that door," Kara pointed outside. "We'll use it as a stretcher."

The hermit started to protest but Kara shot him a withering glance and he snapped his mouth shut.

*   *   *

Kara watched Dez's face while he slept in the Tower's infirmary. He was still pale and thin, but no longer feverish. The sisters had completed the treatment, with her help, and seen to Sarah as well. Sir Toren was laid to rest and Wen would receive his spurs soon. Everything was in order, except for Dez. He was still unconscious. His sister was with Sarina, looking for something to eat in the kitchen so Kara was alone with him. She knelt at his bedside, feeling the cold stone hard on her knees, and prayed like she did every day since their return.

The healer signed quietly and rested her head on the cot next to the warrior. She was exhausted, having refused to leave his side for more than a couple of hours at a time. Her prayers rang through her head in droning repitition. She lost track of how many times she'd said them. Nothing changed. The man still breathed evenly in slumber next to her.

"Come back to us, Dez," she whispered. "Everyone needs you. Your sister and Sarina need you."

"I need you to live, I love you," she said the words in a rush. Words she never dared to say before, like she was afraid if she hesitated, she would never be able to.

"I know we can never be, but I need to know you are alive. It hurts too much to imagine life without you in the world."

She shed no tears, but her voice broke with emotion. Her entire body felt oversensitive, like the time lightning struck close during a storm. That feeling may have been what made her jump, startled when a heavy hand caressed her hair.

"Kara?" Dez's voice was hoarse and weak.

"Blessed Goddess!" Kara cried out and leaped to her feet. "Don't talk, I'll get water."

She ran toward the door, shouting for a passing sister to go get Sarah. She grabbed the pitcher of water and stopped with her back turned to the warrior. Only then did she allow herself to cry. She wondered if he'd heard her confession and what it meant for their future. Had she crossed the line they would be unable to come back from?

She steadied herself and turned to see Dez watching her. That look he always had was there, and something else. Something that made her feel like he knew and accepted whatever she needed. She crossed the room to fill a cup for him. Everything was going to be fine, she knew it.

Relic Hunter: A Wasteland Tale

The lead ball ripped Jule's jacket and cut a burning hole through her shoulder before passing out the back. The pain tore a curse from her throat and she spun back behind the cover of a large stone. She had a matching wound in her thigh and jagged trench along her ribs. She could barely get a breath without pain flaring up somwhere. Each intake of air sent fire through her lungs. Probably a broken rib. She checked her magelock pistol again. Some of her auburn hair had fallen out of the braids that ran along the side of her head and she brushed at them irritably. She had two rounds left in her hand. Two shots, two targets. Her dark eyes searched the sky like it might offer some way out. She'd never been religious, but part of her hoped someone was on her side. She brushed the stray hairs out of her face again. The two braids were tight and connected to one long braid down her back. It usually kept her hair out of her way when she worked. She realized her mind was wandering again. Shock must be setting in, she thought.

"Just leave the bag and we'll forget we saw you," one of the targets shouted from his own cover.

She looked down at her shoulder bag full of relics. Her family needed them to restock their store and survive the Wastes. They could power their home for months on the energy contained in them. Even if she did leave it, she doubted they would let her live. There were four of them originally. One of them was already dead, and another bleeding out in the sand. Her only way out was to get to her skiff and escape. Unfortunately, they were between her and the battered hovercraft.

Another wave of pain lanced up through her body and the edges of her vision blackened. She growled deep in her throat in frustration. She promised her daughter she'd be back soon. Her vision went dark as she fought the nausea that rode in behind that pain.

* * *

"Momma, will you bring me back a gek lizard?"

The little girl bounced around Jules as she lifted the last jug onto the back of her skiff. The liquid inside sloshed as the round container settled on the small craft's deck. Her hand rested briefly on a small dent in the skiff's hull and she smiled. The vehicle was old and built of piecemeal scraps and parts, but she'd had it since she first began scavenging the

Wastes for relics. She'd built it herself from spare parts that her father had lying around the junk depot. He indulged her projects and curiosities and let her use whatever he didn't think he could sell. Since then she'd added more parts and modifications with scraps from her own runs. It was an ugly craft, but it was fast and reliable.

"If I find one, love," Jules said softly.

She secured the last tie down on the small craft and ushered the girl through the back door of the shop nearby. In front, her husband was helping their first customer of the day. She overheard what the customer was looking for and pointed the object out to Tinkla.

"Take that to your father," she said, giving the girl a nudge toward the shelf.

Jules brushed fingers through the girl's mussed brown hair and smiled as her daughter ran off. The woman remembered helping her own father at that age. Life was hard in the Wasteland, and not much easier at the edge of it. Not that the rest of the world was much better, but a life in the Wastes was usually short, dirty, and violent. The people who chose it had a good reason or no other options left. For her and her family, the hardship was made better by the business they'd built. People from nearby communities paid dearly for the relics that Jules dug up in the old ruins scattered throughout the blasted desert. The ancient artifacts contained a power that could be harnessed to run equipment, which made life easier. Water pumps, lights, mills, and even her skiff ran on the power contained in the objects. No one in her time knew where the power came from, but it was life-changing for those who could afford it.

"Tell your father I will be home as soon as I can."

*   *   *

Another crack of a pistol jerked Jules out of the dark abyss she'd been slipping into. The man behind the rock was shouting again but the words made no sense to her. He fired another shot, but she was still behind cover. She realized he was trying to keep her there. The two lead balls were still in her hand and she pushed one into the open breach in her pistol. Looking around the other side of the rock she caught sight of the second man working his way around her flank. She let him keep coming closer, waiting for him to expose himself to rush between two rocks. His friend fired another shot which skipped off the rock above her head. She flinched as dust and rock chips rained down, but she was able to keep her eyes on the gap.

The man made his move and so did Jules. She stood and leveled her weapon, using the rock to stabilize. The other man would be reloading so she'd only have a moment. She sighted along the rune engraved barrel and squeezed the trigger before he reached the middle of the gap. Blue light flared from the fuel compartment as ancient magical energy raced up the runes etched in the handle and chamber of the weapon. The energy exploded out of the chamber and along the barrel, carrying the lead ball with it. She heard him grunt, and a spray of pink mist let her know she'd hit him. She moved before she could see if he went down. She dropped behind cover and another gunshot resulted in a spray of rock chips right where she had been standing.

"Benja?" The man called out to his friend. There was no answer. She heard him curse to himself.

Jules rolled the last round in her fingers while she considered her next move. She'd get one shot at the man. She was wounded, tired, and dizzy from blood loss and the heat from the sun baking the sand under her. If she missed that would be it. She'd lie dead in the Wastes. Her family would lose the shop open and life on Thelos was harsh for people with no way to make a living. She opened the port to load her last round. Her vision swam and she bit her lip to focus, slipping the round into the breach and closed the port. When the port closed the pistol came to life again with a faint blue glow from the relic chamber.

"Benja," the man called again, seeming afraid to leave cover to check on his friend.

She waited for him to call out again, hoping that his attention would be drawn to his downed partner. She pushed up from the sand, fighting the spinning caused by the sudden rush of blood to her head. Biting back nausea, she rushed around the rock and lowered her pistol, sighted, and pulled the trigger. Blue light flared in the relic chamber and rushed along the runes in the gun's handle and combustion chamber. The magelock pistol roared and the light followed the lead ball down the barrel and flashed as it exited, speeding toward its target.

The man fired wildly in return and by the luck of all the Gods his shot missed. Jules saw the flash and heard the shot whistle past. Then he was down, bleeding in the sand. She rush to her vehicle without checking to see if he was alive. Climbing on to her skiff she dug through her shoulder bag to find one of the smaller relics. Finding what she wanted she slapped a panel on the side of the console rising from the flat deck between her feet and dropped in an ancient silver ring. When she closed it the lights on the console flickered to life and a small bluish bar illuminated the panel to her left. She hit a couple of switches and cranked a handle on the side of the steering post but nothing happened.

"Come on girl, we gotta go," Jules spoke to the machine.

She ran her hand over familiar switches, making sure each was in the proper position. Satisfied she flipped the last switch down and back up and returned to the crank. As she turned it she felt a low rumble under the skiff. A puff of dust was forced out from under the back of the vehicle, but then the rumble turned into a whine and then silence.

"We gotta get home," Jules said to herself. Dizziness was setting in again and she rested her forehead against the steering controls. She chanced a glance at the man lying a few feet away. Was he breathing?

She did a slow count to ten under her breath and turned the crank again. This time the sound was promising as the skiff groaned and whined to life. The workings beneath her seat seemed to chug painfully as metal gears and pistons went through the motions of trying to get in sync with each other. Finally, with a belch from an exhaust vent behind her seat the machine growled to life. As the engine settled into a fitful purring Jules slowly pressed a lever forward and the skiff lurched and lifted itself on powerful air currents. After rising about a foot above the ground the vehicle settled into a bobbing hover, awaiting the driver's directions.

"That's my girl," Julies patted the side of the skiff's console fondly.

Jules pushed a lever forward. The vehicle's guts churned louder and pushed them both forward through the air. She turned the hovering skiff away from the men and their own vehicles and toward the flat expanse of the open Wasteland to the east. Dust and sand billowed out from beneath the metal deck and swirled in the wake of the departing craft. Before pushing the accelerator forward to speed off she took one last look back at the scene. The sun's glare on the sand prevented her from seeing much beyond the throbbing redness of pain in her head.

She drove the skiff over the dunes for over an hour, head down and eyes focused on the sand ahead before her injuries forced her to stop. Blood loss and shock were taking their toll and the tunnel vision was getting worse. She was afraid she would crash and lose her only way out of the scorching Wasteland. Pulling the accelerator back Jules brought the skiff to a halt. She threw all the switches off and the craft settled slowly to the sand. Jules turned to step off the vehicle but her knees buckled and she tumbled to the sand. Lying there she could feel the burning of her wounds and knew she needed to take care of them before infection set in.

Jules wanted to sleep, but she fought it back and pulled herself up against the skiff and opened one of the rear compartments. She retrieved a leather satchel and a bottle of clear liquid before settling heavily to the ground. She tried to pull off her jacket but the material was stuck to her shoulder. The dried blood clung to the fabric so she ripped open the seam at the shoulder with the help of her belt knife. With the rest of the jacket now on the ground she could focus on the trapped sleeve. She poured some of the liquid from the bottle over the sleeve, and the wound beneath. She sucked in a breath as it poured over the hole in her shoulder. The liquor they distilled back home was terrible to drink, but perfect for cleaning wounds.

It took her an hour to clean all of her wounds and bind her ribs tightly in cloth torn from her shirt. She had no other clothing to change so looked a ragged sight in pants torn open to the thigh and nothing covering her top half but bandages and the wrap she used around her breasts. She lay in the sand, exhausted and breathing heavy. She knew she had to move again, but she was having trouble finding the energy. Jules reached for her jacket, knowing she had to cover her skin against the blistering sun still high overhead. She got the worn jacket over her as the blackness settled in again.

* * *

Jules pushed the skiff for three days to find the ruin half buried in the sand. She had to range farther to find enough for the shop since her husband had lost his leg. His scavenging days were over so she had to work twice as hard to keep the stock coming in. People traveled for days to buy the antiques that powered their lights, weapons, and comforts. Some people lived in the Wastes to be free, others like Jules lived near it to take what they could. The people that visited their shop were too soft, and too comfortable to enter the Wastes themselves. All their hopes were resting in that old blown-out stone structure with empty windows staring out into Wastes like hollow eyes. The skiff rested on the sunbaked ground behind her and her gear was at her feet. She'd already taken the craft around the perimeter and believed she was alone but she took some time to watch and listen. There were other scavengers who hunted the Wasteland, and many of them were dangerous.

Jules shouldered her pack and put her arm and head through a coil of rope. She checked that her pistol was loaded, then walked up the rise to the ancient ruin. Time and weather buried many of the lower floors beneath the Wasteland. Few people knew why some buildings seemed to survive whatever happened ages ago, but the Wastes were dotted with similar ruins. All stone, tall, and with walls pierced by windows. Historians and scholars, those who had the nerve to travel to the Wasteland, speculated that some smaller buildings may be buried under the dunes, those that survived anyway. It was these exposed ruins that drew the scavengers and relic hunters like Jules.

When she reached the top of the hill where the ground met the walls of the ruin, she would have to climb up through one of the windows. She hesitated, listening again before going up into the dark. There were no sounds inside so she grabbed the concrete ledge above and pulled herself up over the sill of the opening. Jules crouched in the patch of sunlight coming through the gap in the stone and pulled her pack around. She took out a small lantern and a tool to light it. They had lanterns powered by relics at the shop but they needed to conserve the fuel. She could spare the energy or the little tool that made a tiny flame, however.

"Now let's see if you were worth it," Jules whispered to the building.

She stood up and gathered her things. Stepping into the shadows brought the temperature down considerably. All around her, as far as the lantern light would reach, were rows of columns holding up the floor above. Most large ruins were like this. Hollow stone structures whose use was long lost to the ages. All around were scattered piles of debris, ancient furniture, and evidence that walls had once divided the floor into rooms. Each room surrounded by a metal frame whose skin had been blasted away or rotted under time's steady hand. She started her search right away.

Hours passed and only a few trinkets had found their way into her pack. Mostly small pieces used to power hand-held lights or timepieces.

She would need more than that to power the skiff home. She had a decision to make. The floors above may hold something substantial, but she knew where to find larger treasure. Every ruin of that size had large machinery on the bottom floors. The sorts of machines that would need large, expensive relics to function. It would take her below ground level and out of earshot of anyone who might come along while she was down there. Something more dangerous that scavengers may also have made its home below. After all that, the lower floors might be buried and it would simply be a waste of time.

She finally came to a decision and headed toward what she hoped was an intact stairwell. She found it in the corner of the building. A dark doorway led to stone stairs that wound up and down the inside walls. Both directions were dark and silent, and she was relieved to see that the first few flights were clear. By the smell of it bats had taken up residence somewhere above, but she detected no other signs of life. She held the lantern over the open pit in the center of the chamber but its light was too dim for her to see anything. She'd have to descend.

Jules moved down the stairs. The old stone was crumbling in places. Corners of the steps broke away under her feet and there was no railing between her and the open chasm in the center. There may have once been a handrail but it was long since lost to time. With each turn, she expected to find the passage blocked, or stairwell collapsed but it remained clear.

Finally, she set foot on the solid ground of the building deep beneath the dunes above.

The air was cold and stale, and her lantern did little to cut through the darkness around her. She got the sense that she was in a large open area and for the moment it was oppressively quiet. She stood still, straining her ears to pick up anything. Nothing moved or made a sound. She pulled a small white stone out of her pocket and marked an X on the wall at the bottom of the stairs. She might find other exits, but this would let her know which one definitely reached the surface.

Satisfied with her mark she put her right hand on the wall and walked into the dark with the glow of the lantern reaching out a few feet in front of her. The floor was somewhere below a layer of sand and debris blown down from the floors above. Despite her best efforts to move silently, her boots scraped on stone and she stopped every few feet to see if the noise caused a response from somewhere in the dark. Still nothing moved, and finally, she found what she was looking for. Her light played across the surface of a large metal hulk rising from the floor. Its purpose was long lost to time, but Jules could tell that it had moving parts. Moving parts meant power.

Jules searched the outside of the machine for any compartment marked with the sign the ancients used to denote power. The signs rarely survived the ravages of time, and this was one of those cases. She'd have to remove the panels to find the relic. She retrieved her tools and set to work. Within an hour she found the relic powering that machine, and two machines nearby. Her bag was full and she had enough to get home with plenty to spare. Her haul would keep the shop going another few weeks, and now she knew where to find more.

She secured her bag, picked up her lantern, and put her other hand against the nearby wall to reverse her course back to the stairs. The climb back to the surface was slower than her descent thanks to the weight of her cargo. She kept her hand on the wall to her left and her ears strained to detect any sound other than her breathing or the wind. Time became a mystery in the bowels of the ruin. Jules knew someone, or something, else could have come along in that time.

"Wake up," a voice called in the dark ahead. "Momma, wake up."

"Tinkla?" What was her daughter doing in the basement with her?

"Wake up!"

The voice was louder, insistent...male.

* * *

Jules snapped awake and panic burst in her mind as she found herself unable to move. There was a weight on her chest and arms, pinning her to the ground. She looked up into the glare and saw the silhouette of someone looming over her. It was the man she'd left bleeding in the sand, ragged and tattered with his left arm hanging limp from a gruesome wound in his shoulder.

"There you are," he smiled his broken-toothed smile and the rancid stink of his breath rolled over her as he leaned close.

She gagged and struggled but his weight held her firm. His smile widened as she tried to twist under him.

"You're going to pay for my men, and for my arm ya filthy leech."

He figured she was from outside the Wasteland. People who lived their lives in the Wastes were territorial people and hated relic hunters from outside coming in and taking artifacts. He traced a finger along her chin and down her neck. He'd tossed her jacket away while she slept and the rough ground bit into her back as she struggled harder. His finger reached the wrap around her breasts and he tugged at it but the material held fast while the loose end was trapped under her back.

She was filled with anger and revulsion at his touch. Her skin crawled wherever he made contact and a boiling hate rose from her gut at the thought of what he was planning. There was also shame. Shame that she had been caught unaware and that she had left him alive. When he reached the tops of her breasts that anger burst into a rage but she tamped it down when she realized the same thing he did. There was little he could do to her the way he had her pinned, except kill her maybe. That would be preferable to what she imagined was on his mind. She made herself relax and stop struggling. She pushed away the shame and revulsion, but she stoked that rage like low hot coals. Tiny motes of red-hot fire under white ash waiting for a breath to bring the flames forth again.

"Now don't you move," he commanded.

He drew a boot knife and clamped it between his teeth to free up his good hand. The threat was clear as he shifted his weight down her body. His knees left her arms but she waited. He sat across her hips, pinning her legs to the ground.

"Don't move," he growled around the knife.

She waited. Her wounds were on fire and the rocks under her legs and back felt like glass on her skin. He grabbed roughly at her breast, digging his filthy fingers into her flesh. She watched his eyes. She waited. He dug the fingers of his good hand under her chest wrap. Her skin crawled with revulsion. She waited. He pushed his entire hand under the tight wrapping and found his goal. His calloused hand dug painfully into the sensitive parts of her breast.

She'd waited long enough. That revulsion, pain, and anger came boiling to the surface under the raging inferno in her belly. With a scream like some wild beast going in for the kill she swung her fist toward the side of his head. He jerked up, but his hand was trapped by his own lustful folly. He dodged the blow, but not completely. Her forearm connected with his mouth, which still held the knife clamped in his rotting teeth. The blade sank deep into his face, and her bare arm. The pain lanced through her body but she used it to drive her, thrusting her hips and throwing the screaming man off her. The blade fell to the ground near her hand as he rolled away clutching at his face.

Jules rolled onto her side and pushed herself to her hands and knees. Her body ached and her wounds were like liquid fire under her skin. She picked up the knife and got to her feet, gritting her teeth against the pain. Her forearm bled freely where the blade opened her bare skin and blood dripped from her fingers into the hot sand at her feet. The wounded man scrambled away, still clutching at his ruined face.

"I just wanted to get home to my family," Jules growled. She kicked him, connecting hard with his ribs.

"Why did you have to stop at that ruin?" She aimed another kick at him.

This time he rolled toward her and they both went down in a tangle. He was fighting half blinded by the blood on his face but managed to get his arms around her. She could barely move but managed to get the knife turned toward his stomach and drive it home. He looked surprised when she felt the weapon's hilt pressed against his body. His hold on her relaxed. She twisted the blade and he coughed, spraying blood and spittle across her cheek. He slipped from the knife and to the ground and she watched his last gurgling breaths as the light died in his eyes.

"I just want to see my girl," she said softly as the blade fell to the sand.

Jules used the last scrap of her shirt to bind her arm and found her jacket nearby. She pulled the worn leather over her shoulders and sighed in the comfort of its embrace. She stumbled toward her skiff and retrieved her discarded satchel, ensuring the contents were still safe inside. Jules strapped the bag to the back of her skiff and when she was done she raised her eyes to meet those of a small reptile.

She had no idea where the creature came from, or when it had taken up residence on her skiff. The little gek lizard regarded her calmly from the worn leather seat. Its frilled neck was red against the green of its scaly body. The little creature regarded her with large eyes, its head tilted slightly as if curious about her. She reached for the creature and it showed no fear as she carefully picked it up and cupped it in her hands.

"Come, my little friend, we're going home."

Made in the USA
Columbia, SC
27 August 2019